M000031811

"What happened to the water?"
Annie yelled.

It was all Marsh could do to keep from laughing at her predicament. She was wrapped in an oversize terry robe, her hair a halo of shampoo bubbles, her feet dripping sudsy water on the wooden floor. "You don't have water?"

"No, I don't. Nor do I have a towel." She swiped at her eyes with the sleeve of her robe, then threw up her hands in agitation, launching a handful of soap bubbles into the air.

That did it. Marsh howled with laughter.

She lunged for him, but he captured her hands, pinning them to his chest. When she struggled, he engulfed her in his arms and hefted her up until she was nose to nose with him, her eyes wide, her mouth an O of surprise.

And then, giving in to the proximity of those pretty lips, he kissed her....

Dear Reader,

This month we're proud to present our Premiere title for 1993—it's a wonderful love story called *Still Sweet on Him,* by an exciting new author, Jodi O'Donnell.

Jodi, a native of Iowa, has written a romance from the heart, set in a place much like her own hometown. This book was also the winner of the 1992 Golden Heart Award given by the Romance Writers of America for an outstanding unpublished novel. Look for Jodi's special letter to you in the front pages of *Still Sweet on Him.*

If you enjoy this book—and we hope you do!—look for Jodi's next book, *The Farmer Takes a Wife,* coming in February 1994.

Our popular FABULOUS FATHERS series continues this month with *Mad About Maggie,* by one of your favorite authors, Pepper Adams. And don't forget to visit Duncan, Oklahoma—where love can make miracles happen—as Arlene James's THIS SIDE OF HEAVEN trilogy continues with *An Old-Fashioned Love.*

Look for more great romances this month by Maris Soule, Marcy Gray and Linda Varner. This month and every month, we're dedicated to bringing you heartwarming, exciting love stories. Your comments and suggestions are important to us. Please write and tell us about the books and authors you enjoy best.

Happy reading!

Anne Canadeo
Senior Editor
Silhouette Romance

FIRELIGHT AND FOREVER
Linda Varner

Silhouette
ROMANCE™
Published by Silhouette Books New York
America's Publisher of Contemporary Romance

Special thanks to Elizabeth A. Moseley, RN, who came back from vacation with a "great idea" that really was!

SILHOUETTE BOOKS
300 East 42nd St., New York, N.Y. 10017

FIRELIGHT AND FOREVER

Copyright © 1993 by Linda Varner Palmer

ISBN: 0-373-08966-X

First Silhouette Books printing October 1993

Books by Linda Varner

Silhouette Romance

Heart of the Matter #625
Heart Rustler #644
Luck of the Irish #665
Honeymoon Hideaway #698
Better To Have Loved #734
A House Becomes a Home #780
Mistletoe and Miracles #835
As Sweet as Candy #851
Diamonds Are Forever #868
A Good Catch #906
Something Borrowed #943
Firelight and Forever #966

LINDA VARNER

definitely believes in love at first sight. "But Jim and I were only in ninth grade when we fell, so a whirlwind courtship was definitely out of the question!" Today, she remains happily married to her junior high school sweetheart, and they live in their Arkansas hometown with their two children.

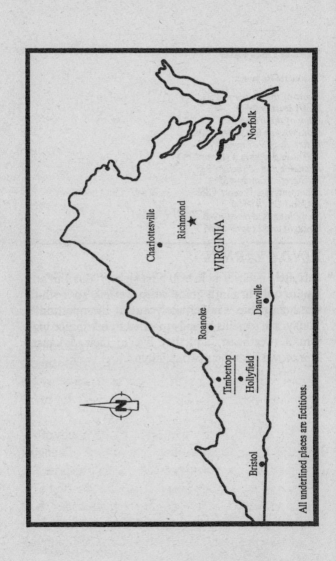

VIRGINIA

Norfolk

Charlottesville
Richmond

Roanoke
Danville

Timbertop
Hollyfield

Bristol

All underlined places are fictitious.

Prologue

The familiar creak of the storage shed door drew Hal Roth to the open window of his second-story study. He looked out over Timbertop, the youth camp he and his wife, Opal, had built together some twenty-odd years ago, and spotted Marshal McGriffey, a former camper who now worked as a counselor. A perpetual camera suspended from a strap around his neck, sixteen-year-old Marsh selected a cane fishing pole from the many stored in that old shed.

Clearly he'd elected to spend his two hours of afternoon free time alone at the lake instead of hanging out with the other counselors. That didn't surprise Hal one bit, and he shook his head, not for the first time very concerned about this solemn teenager he'd learned to love like a son through the years.

It was almost as if Marsh clothed himself in invisible, invincible armor so nothing and no one could touch him. . . .

"Marsh!"

Both Hal and his young counselor jumped in surprise at the sudden cry. Hal followed the sound and discovered a stray camper, Annie Winslow, hurtling herself down the path from the recreation building where all the others busied themselves with arts and crafts. Nine years old, as mischievous as her hair was red, Annie was one of the orphans Hal took in every summer on a charity basis. She would be at Timbertop until the state found her a foster home.

"What's this?" Marsh demanded of Annie, his words clearly audible to Hal. "Aren't you supposed to be with the other girls, making a bird cage out of clothespins or something?"

"Oh, that's for sissies," she replied, wrinkling her freckled nose with distaste. "And I don't have no bird, nohow. I have a turtle." She eyed the cane poles in the shed behind him. "Are you going fishing?"

"What does it look like?" Marsh retorted, snatching out a pole and quickly shutting the door.

"Can I come with you?"

"Nope." He picked up a battered coffee can, most likely filled with dirt and worms.

"I'll bait my own hook," Annie promised, hopping first on one sneakered foot, then the other.

"No, thanks."

"And I'll bait yours, too."

"I said no." Marsh shifted his load so he could pick up his tackle box. That done, he pivoted toward the lake, managing one whole step before Annie flung herself directly into his path, arms outstretched to halt him.

"Will you take me if I give you my arrowhead?" she asked, hastily adding, "It's real."

"No, Annie."

"I have a white rock. Found it at the creek."

"No."

Annie hesitated, as though in a quandary, then seemed to come to a decision. "You can have my turtle."

"No!" Marsh veered around her and took another step in the direction of the lake. Annie grabbed his arm, a move that threatened to dump the worms on the rocky path.

"But you have to take me with you," she cried. "You have to."

Hal, who heard every word of their exchange, tensed, not sure what to expect now. Though Marsh might be a good kid, he was no saint, and he certainly had every right to lose his cool with this pesky orphan no one seemed to want.

"And just *why* do I have to take you fishing?" Marsh demanded.

"'Cause if you don't, who will?" Annie answered, tipping her head back to look up at him with doleful eyes. The breeze ruffled her cap of copper curls and billowed under the oversized T-shirt that skimmed the top of decidedly knobby knees.

Long silence followed her reply—silence that seemed to say Marsh might actually be considering the request. Then the youth heaved a lusty sigh, a sound that the wind carried right up to Hal.

"I'll get another pole," the teenager said.

Annie whooped her glee, while high above, Hal clutched the windowsill to help support his shell-shocked knees. Astonished, he watched Marsh head back the few steps to the shed, Annie skipping circles around him. Once Marsh reached the door, he handed her the tackle box and worm can, then leaned his own pole up against the building.

"Did you dig these yourself?" she asked, peering into the can as Marsh rummaged around in the shed.

"Yes."

"Do the fish like them?"

"Yes."

"Are there any big ones in that lake?"

"Yes."

"Can we keep them?"

With another sigh, Marsh stepped back and turned to his companion. "We'll give them to Miss Opal. Now you get one more question, then you have to be quiet. Good fishermen don't talk."

Annie stood in silence, evidently trying to decide what to ask.

Obviously relishing the moment of peace, Marsh relieved her of the tackle box and worms. Then, unbelievably, he grinned at her. "Well? What's it going to be?"

Annie tilted her head to one side. Solemnly she gazed at him. "Is Marsh short for marshmallow?" she finally asked.

Clearly surprised by her question, Marsh said nothing for a millisecond. Then he threw his head back and laughed—*laughed*—a magical sound that brought tears to Hal's eyes.

"Must be," Marsh told Annie, ruffling her wild curls.

"Neat-o," she commented, taking the pole he handed her. "I like marshmallows—'specially when they're roasted."

"So do I," her companion said as, together, they headed toward the lake.

Stunned to his toes by what he'd witnessed, Hal stared after them. His heart swelled with love and new hope for Marsh, and he sent a thank-you heavenward for the rambunctious, red-haired sprite who'd somehow seen through this loner's gruff camouflage right to his soul . . . as soft as a marshmallow.

Chapter One

"Can you hold on a second, Pops? There's someone at the door."

At Hal Roth's affirmative, Annie Winslow lay the telephone receiver on the bar and made a beeline for the screen door upon which someone—a tall, broad-shouldered someone—had just knocked.

"Hi, there," she said as she flung the door open and motioned the stranger inside Hal's kitchen. "Are you here to repair the dishwasher, the well pump or the roof?"

The man, now standing just inside the room, ran his fingers through chestnut hair that was already tousled enough and glanced back at the unlocked door.

"None of the above, actually," he said, giving her a look of censure. "And that means you should be a bit more cautious about inviting strangers in—" He broke off rather abruptly and narrowed his gaze at her. "Are you... Annie? Little Annie Winslow?"

Annie froze and stared right back, frantically searching through her memory for this ruggedly handsome face. She found a younger version of it almost instantly and gasped her recognition. "Marsh McGriffey!"

He nodded.

"Oh, my God." At once, the past eighteen years of life and living fell away. Annie was nine again and face-to-face with the counselor she idolized. Naturally she squealed and flung herself at him, throwing her arms around his neck in a bear hug.

Marsh wheezed his surprise and stumbled backward against the door, taking her with him. Only after he regained his balance did he return the hug, rather reluctantly in Annie's opinion. Not in the least perturbed about that, Annie just hugged him all the harder before finally stepping back.

"Gosh, it's good to see you," she exclaimed, grasping his shoulders, raising and then lowering her gaze to sweep every precious inch of him.

"It's, um, good to see you, too," Marsh murmured. He eyed her with much less enthusiasm, and it was all Annie could do not to laugh. She'd forgotten how very reserved he was. "Where's Hal?"

"You haven't heard? He's in the— Oh, my goodness!" Whirling, Annie snatched up the phone. "Pops? Are you still there?"

"Still here," replied the man whose kindness had earned him her eternal loyalty and love.

"I'm so sorry. I was...we were..." She bubbled with laughter. "You'll never guess who just walked through your door."

"Marsh McGriffey, from the sound of things," Hal replied with a good-natured chuckle, adding, "And it's about time. Let me talk to him."

About time? Puzzled by Hal's comment—was he expecting an appearance from his former counselor?—Annie automatically handed the phone to Marsh, then dashed out of the kitchen and down the hall to the bathroom.

There, she peered into the mirror over the sink, groaning her disgust before turning on the tap, which sputtered ominously and finally delivered a trickle of cold water. Annie splashed what she could onto her dirt-smudged cheeks, then tried to restore order to the long, naturally curly hair that had always been hard to tame and which, after this morning's work scouring the dorms, looked positively wild.

Why she even bothered, Annie couldn't imagine. She'd certainly never worried about her appearance before, but then, she'd been nine years old the last time she'd seen him. At twenty-seven now, she naturally wanted to look nice, a desire that had nothing to do with Marsh and everything to do with womanhood.

"Annie?" It was her guest, no doubt wondering where in the world she'd gone.

"Be right there," she called, a second later joining Marsh in the kitchen. She took note of his empty hands and glanced toward the phone on the bar. Turning back to him, Annie arched an eyebrow in silent questioning.

"Hal said he'd talk to both of us this afternoon at the hospital," Marsh said. He shook his head, clearly bemused. "How long has he been laid up?"

"Since Monday."

"And his knee surgery is scheduled for when?"

"Actually, it hasn't been scheduled yet."

"Oh." He said nothing else, and seconds of silence stretched to minutes.

"Would you—"

"May I—"

They both laughed rather self-consciously.

"You first," Marsh prompted.

"I was just going to offer you a chair," Annie said. "And something to drink or eat or...whatever." She shrugged. "As the saying goes, if I'd known you were coming I'd have baked a cake. But since I didn't know, we'll have to make do with whatever we can scrounge up. I haven't had time to go to the grocery store yet."

"I take it Hal sent you a telegram, too?"

Annie frowned. "You mean he wired you?"

Marsh nodded. "On Tuesday. Told me to 'come at once,' so of course I did." Of course. Though Annie hadn't seen Marsh in eighteen years, she knew that he and Hal had kept in touch and were actually quite close. "Tell me what happened."

"We were trying to fix the leak in the roof. He lost his balance and slid right down the north side." She closed her eyes, for a moment reliving the horror. "I thought he was a goner. Luckily, he landed in the hedgerow. No broken bones. Just bruises, scratches and those torn ligaments in his knee."

"Then you were already here at Timbertop when it happened?"

"That's right. I came on Sunday." She lifted her chin and gave him a proud grin. "You're looking at the new camp nurse."

"Ah." He gave that a moment's thought. "So you're a nurse. I'm not surprised. You always had a knack for healing little hurts."

"Little hurts, huh? Well, that explains why I was so miserable working in the emergency room."

He winced. "I'm sorry. I really wasn't insulting your abilities."

"Of course not," she said, and motioned him to a bar stool. "How could you when you know so little about them? Now, would you like a cola or some iced tea?"

"Tea, please," he replied rather meekly, perching on one of the swivel stools.

"I could make you a sandwich. We do have bologna." She walked over to the refrigerator and peered inside. "I see salami, too. Oops. Forget the salami. It's green."

Marsh actually laughed. "I ate in Mountainburg barely an hour ago."

"At Brook's Barbecue?"

"How'd you guess?"

"Some things never change," she teased, well remembering his penchant for the spicy sandwiches made by one of the locals.

"Some *things*, maybe. But I know a some*one* who has. You're all grown up, Annie Winslow." It was his turn to make inspection, and she found herself squirming as his gaze traveled slowly over her.

Quickly Annie turned her back on him. Disconcerted, wishing she weren't so bony, she snatched down two large glasses from the cabinet. After filling them with ice, she added a generous portion of Hal's famous lemon tea and handed a glass to Marsh. She then took a fortifying swallow from her own before attempting to refill the ice tray.

"Darn pump," she muttered under her breath when a twist of the faucet failed to produce even a drop of water.

"What's wrong?"

"It only works when it wants to these days." Annie turned to explain and found herself eye-to-Adam's apple with Marsh—a shock since she hadn't heard him leave his seat. "S-someone is supposed to come out to fix it. At least that's what they promised. Heaven knows they'd better. The cook and counselors are due on Saturday, and we'll have campers on Sunday." Annie got a sudden whiff of Marsh's spicy after-shave. At once intensely aware of his proximity, she swept past, drink in hand, and walked over to sit on the bar stool farthest from the one he'd chosen moments before.

"Are you telling me that Hal intends to open up as planned?" He looked incredulous.

"The man hasn't missed a summer in forty-five years—not even last year, right after Opal died. Did you really think a little thing like knee surgery would stop him?"

"But who's going to run the place until he's up and about?"

"You?" Annie asked, suddenly wondering if she'd hit upon the reason Hal would wire Marsh to "come at once." Independent in the extreme, it wasn't at all like that dear old man to send for someone just to hold his hand during a relatively minor, if incapacitating, surgical procedure. Marsh's jaw dropped. "I can't hang around here all summer. I'm in the middle of a project."

Annie, who'd just this week perused Hal's collection of Marsh's work smiled her sympathy and—she had to admit it—her relief. She planned on managing the camp herself during Hal's absence. Was looking forward to it, in fact.

"Don't worry. If that's really what he has in mind, I'll talk him out of it. And as for Timbertop, I'm sure I can keep things going until he's on his feet again. Why, the place should run itself. Besides, Ms. Potter, the cook—"

"*She's* still here?"

"Yes, and just as spry as ever. Between her and the four counselors, all of whom are also old pros, we'll be able to handle anything—even carting water from the lake, if we have to."

"Want me to take a look at the pump?" Marsh asked from his vantage point by the sink. He had his back to her and stared out the window, raised to lure the late May breeze. Annie didn't know if he was looking at the well house or beyond it to the cabins nestled into the hillside.

Only two of those six buildings served as dormitories these days...thank goodness. There was a time when Timbertop sheltered as many as fifty kids at once.

"Think you can fix it?"

"Who knows? I'm usually pretty good at that sort of thing."

And a few others, I'll bet, Annie thought as he crossed over to his drink and downed it in one swallow. Wiping the back of his hand across his mouth, Marsh headed toward the back door.

"Tools still in the shed?" he asked over his shoulder.

Annie, disturbed by the crazy direction of her thoughts, barely heard him. "The... Oh, uh, yes. Same as always."

The moment Marsh stepped out the door and out of sight, Annie finished off her own drink and then slowly trailed him as far as the back porch. From there, she watched as he vanished into the shed and then emerged again, old metal toolbox in hand, to walk to the well house.

Annie noted with interest the easy grace of his long-legged stride. Marsh had grown a good six inches since last she saw him. He looked very fit, she thought, and confident. Had his stint in the military done that for him? Or his subsequent success as a photojournalist?

Whatever the reason, he appeared fully capable of handling anything and anyone, except—she smiled slightly at the memory of their hug—a certain redhead, who didn't know what to make of him, either.

"Did you call the plumber and cancel the repair?" Hal asked Annie three hours later that day. A patient in the Hollyfield Memorial Hospital, located twenty miles from Timbertop, he lay in an orthopedic bed, knee elevated and packed on ice.

"With pleasure, and I put the dishwasher repairman on hold," Annie replied, smoothing the crisp white sheet that covered her boss. "Marsh did such a good job on the well pump, I wrangled a promise that he'd look at the dishwasher, too."

Hal nodded his approval. "Thanks, son. I knew you wouldn't let me down," he said to Marsh.

Annie and Marsh exchanged a look. She noted the barest hint of a frown knitting his brow and knew he still wondered why Hal had sent for him. So did she.

"How's the knee?" she asked.

"Doc can't get the swelling down and can't operate until he does. Looks like I may be stuck here awhile." He turned to Marsh, standing on the opposite side of the bed. "That's why I wired you. Twenty-four campers are due to arrive at Timbertop on Sunday. Annie's going to have her hands full seeing after their scrapes and bruises. Cook's going to be up to her neck in bacon, eggs and biscuits. My counselors are good, but green yet . . . too green to manage the place. I need someone with experience and maturity to stand in for me. I need you, Marsh."

"But, Pops," Annie interjected, when Marsh didn't immediately reply. "You can't expect him to put his life on hold and move to Timbertop. He's a famous photographer. Why, I'll bet he's in the middle of a project right now." She raised her questioning gaze to Marsh, silently prompting him to jump in anytime.

He cleared his throat. "As a matter of fact, I am."

"Hot damn!" The silver-haired man positively beamed. He shifted his gaze to Annie. "Marsh has won awards for his work."

"You told me."

"I have all his books."

"You showed me."

Hal grinned at Marsh. "Congratulations. I'm proud of you."

"Thanks."

"Don't worry about Timbertop," he continued, much to Annie's relief. "I'll find someone else to manage the place. You get on back home and get busy on that new book. What's this one about, by the way?"

"The faces of age."

Hal winced. "Want me to model for you? It's the least I can do after dragging you all the way to Virginia."

"Thanks, but you're not old enough," Marsh smoothly replied, words that put a smile on his friend's face.

Hal then changed the subject. Management of Timbertop was not mentioned again in the thirty minutes Annie and Marsh spent with him, nor when they left.

Annie knew Hal still worried about it, though. She could almost see the wheels of conjecture turning in his brain, no doubt trying to produce the name of some other long-lost counselor on whom he could call.

That rankled. Didn't he realize she could handle management of Timbertop alone?

If a thoughtful Annie said little during the thirty-minute drive home, her handsome companion said less. The moment she parked the car and killed the engine, she hopped out and headed straight indoors to the telephone.

"Who are you calling?" Marsh asked when he entered the kitchen a few moments later.

"The dishwasher repairman," she told him. "I know you need to get on home, and there's simply no need for you to hang around here just to work on it."

"I figured as much." Marsh snatched the receiver from her ear and dropped it into the cradle. "I told you I'd fix the thing, and I will."

"But your book—"

"Can wait one more day." Marsh sat on one of the bar stools. He patted the one next to him, inviting Annie to do the same. "Sit. We need to talk."

With a shrug and some unexplainable reluctance, Annie did as requested.

"You want to manage Timbertop for Hal, don't you?"

"How'd you guess?" Annie asked, surprised that he had read her so easily.

"Never mind that," he replied. "What do you know about running a camp?"

"Not that much, but how hard can it be?"

Marsh laughed. "Let me put it this way—I've seen Opal ready to murder Hal, the counselors, the cook and all fifty campers."

Annie gulped audibly. "Sweet Opal Roth? Ready to murder?"

Marsh nodded solemnly. "There are any number of things that can go wrong while camp is in session, and, from my own experience, most of them will. While I was a counselor here, I witnessed four near drownings, two fires, two—no, three lost campers, four broken legs, two broken arms, countless sprains, a poison-ivy epidemic, a snake bite and one very hostile mama bear looking for the cub one of our campers had adopted."

"Good grief! Sounds like a weekend in the ER...minus the bear, of course."

"Exactly. Are you sure you want to be the person in charge?"

"Well, I..." Annie heaved a sigh. "Actually, now that I think about it, maybe not. I just don't want Hal to lay up there in that hospital bed and worry himself sicker, you know?"

"I do know, and I don't want that any more than you do." Marsh frowned. "Surely there's someone else we could call. Some counselor who worked here as long as I did...." He thought for a moment. "How about Ronnie White? Wasn't he from this area?"

"Yes, but he's a county deputy now and—"

"Wouldn't be free to devote a whole summer to Timbertop? Probably not, and neither would most other possibles."

"Actually, if Hal's surgery goes well, he'll be home in no time and anxious to be back in charge. I don't think we'll need a substitute manager for more than two weeks, three tops."

"Yeah?"

"Yeah." Annie took note of his thoughtful expression and, suddenly inspired, asked, "When is your book due in?"

"I promised my publisher he'd have something in three months."

"Hmm. Think you can spare a couple of weeks to help a poor old man who loves you like crazy?"

"There's nothing I'd rather do," Marsh said. "But there's no way that I can. No way at all." He said the words with conviction, but Annie noticed he wouldn't meet her probing gaze.

That apparent unease told her he felt more than a little guilt about his answer, and though eager to send him on his way, Annie was too loyal to Hal to ignore what appeared to be a golden opportunity to recruit Marsh.

"Are you sure? He'd be so grateful."

"I'm very sure," Marsh said. "I have work I must do. I can't do it here, Hal or no." Abruptly he got to his feet and walked over to the sink. There he tested first the hot water, then the cold.

Relentlessly, Annie followed. "You could stay if you did a book on the faces of *youth* instead of *age*. Why, in less than a week the place will be crawling with models."

"No, Annie."

"You could manage the camp—"

"No."

"And take photographs at the same time."

"No."

"The perfect solution to our problem."

"No!"

Annie waited for the echo of his yell to die down before continuing her onslaught against his guilty conscience. "Please stay, Marsh. You just have to."

"And why is that?" he retorted in visible exasperation.

Sensing imminent victory, Annie fumbled through her brain for the perfect reply, then grinned when she suddenly remembered the magic words. "Because if you don't, who will?"

Marsh caught his breath and glared at her. "That may have worked on a soft-hearted sixteen-year-old, Annie, but it won't work now."

Oh, yeah? "Then I guess that's that." Sighing dramatically, Annie walked back to the bar and perched on the stool once again, shoulders slumped. "I'm disappointed, of course, but I understand, really. As for Hal...you know he only wants what's best for you. That's why he's given so freely of his time and talents all these years. Wasn't he the one who first put a camera into your hands?"

"Don't do this to me, Annie."

"Do what?" She gave him a sweet smile.

Marsh groaned in response. "I don't have time to hang out here at Timbertop."

"Maybe not," Annie replied. "But you'd never, ever regret it."

Dead silence followed that prediction, then Marsh uttered a four-letter word that would have earned him a bowl of soap soup if Miss Opal had been around to hear it.

"Does that mean you're going to stay?" Annie asked, barely containing a victory *whoop!*

"You know it does."

She beamed at him. "Thanks a million, Marsh."

"You may as well call me marsh*mallow*," he muttered. "Apparently where y—I mean, Hal is concerned, that's all I'll ever be."

Chapter Two

Seconds later, Marsh slipped off to his Jeep to get his gear. As he hauled his duffel bag out of the back seat, he considered his promise to stay around Timbertop for a few weeks. Instantly he wished he hadn't made that promise, and not because he didn't want to help Hal.

Marsh loved Hal dearly—would have died for him, in fact. He was the father Marsh never knew, just as Timbertop was the loving home Marsh's own kin never provided. Marsh did not intend that either Hal or the camp should come to any harm...especially if he could prevent it.

So why his reluctance to stay? And why did his stomach now churn with the certainty of a bad decision? Marsh knew there was one reason and one reason only: Annie Winslow.

As a child, she touched his heart in ways no other person could. As a fully grown woman, she still had the knack, and he knew instinctively that could mean trouble for a loner such as he.

An expert in avoiding emotional entanglement, Marsh hated the tender feelings she invariably kindled within him. He felt oddly self-conscious around her—unsure of himself, off balance.

Vulnerable.

With a soft grunt of disgust, Marsh flung the heavy canvas bag over his shoulder and turned back toward the house, his thoughts on the mysterious power Annie Winslow held over him. When he raised his gaze to the porch, he saw the woman in question standing there in the doorway like some red-haired sorceress, holding the screen back so he could walk inside.

At once, his heart did a sort of flip, and Marsh stopped short, damned reluctant to enter her enchanted castle.

Enchanted castle? *Get a grip!* Squaring his shoulders, Marsh took the steps two at a time, then brushed right on by her to walk into the room, which was only Opal's old kitchen, after all. Whirling around, he reaffirmed that his hostess was no witch, but just Annie—slender as a reed, with no magic up her sleeve.

"I'm so glad you're staying," she said as she closed the door behind them. "It can get awfully lonely around here. I don't know how Hal stands it in the winter when there aren't any campers about."

Lonely? She'd been lonely? Marsh knew all about lonely and didn't wish it on anyone, most of all on Annie.

"Where should I put my things?" he asked, his voice clipped with irritation. Again, she'd managed to touch him, to make him feel. And he'd been on his guard, too.

"Right this way," Annie replied, and led him down the hall to the stairs. Each aged wooden step creaked as they progressed upward to the second floor. Once there, Annie motioned for him to follow her down another wide hall to a closed door. She twisted the tarnished brass knob and gave it a little push, revealing a massive bedroom filled with furniture as old and dignified as the house.

"The bath is behind that door there. My bedroom is just beyond that, so we'll be sharing it—" Annie suddenly blushed a pretty shade of pink. "The bath, I mean. We'll be sharing the bath."

Marsh stood speechless, his thoughts ricocheting from sharing a bed to sharing a bath.

"Actually, what we're going to share is the bath-*room*," Annie said, as though reading his errant thoughts. "And now that we have that straight—" she bubbled with laughter "—why don't I just open these drapes and let in some sunshine.... Listen! Can you hear that bluebird? Hal loves them, you know. Why, he's nailed a bird box to every tree."

"I saw."

Annie turned back around, smiled at Marsh, then gave the room a quick inspection. "Is there anything else you need?"

"Can't think of a thing."

"Then I'll skedaddle. I've got to make a run into town for a few groceries. Will you be okay here alone until I get back?"

"I'll be fine," Marsh told her.

What he could have said was, "I'll be better," for standing by the window with the sunshine at her back, Annie didn't look so very slender after all. In fact, she looked quite curvaceous in silhouette, not to mention sexy as hell. With a start, Marsh realized that the response she evoked from him was not simply emotional, but physical, as well.

That discovery—made the hard way—shocked him so that he actually hid in his room until he saw her drive from the camp a short time later. Then and only then did he walk downstairs and straight out the door, breathing in deeply the clear air for which the Virginia Blue Ridge Highlands were famous.

That air did wonders to blow the cobwebs from Marsh's brain and ease the tension from his body. As a result, his spirits lifted and he found himself whistling an old 'round-the-campfire tune he hadn't thought of in years.

With a chuckle at the other memories suddenly flooding his head, Marsh finally headed to the chow hall, wherein he and countless other campers had dined. On first glance, it looked exactly the same. On second, Marsh found the huge room dreadfully rundown.

Water stains marbled the high wooden ceiling and the painted walls, indicative of old—or were they new?—leaks. The planks that made up the floor dipped slightly in the aisles, worn down by the trampling of hundreds of feet.

Shaking his head in his distress, Marsh walked over to the nearest table and immediately recognized it as one that he, himself, had sat at in the past. Carved into its wooden surface, he actually found his initials entwined with those of many other campers.

No new furniture in all these years? Marsh couldn't believe it, just as he couldn't believe the dishwasher when he stepped into the kitchen.

It looked to be one of the first ever made, and after a quick inspection, Marsh realized he would never be able to repair it. The manufacturer had gone out of business years ago, making replacement parts an impossibility.

Disturbed by the sad state of the dishwasher, Marsh next checked out the stove and refrigerator. They both looked a bit newer, and on closer examination, appeared to be functional, but Marsh couldn't help but wonder about the rest of Timbertop.

Turning on his heel, he strode to the door, fully intending to take a walk through the camp to survey the dormitories. But just as he stepped outside, Annie called out to him.

"Marsh? Where are you?"

"Over here," he called back, startled that she had made it back already. A quick glance at his watch revealed that he'd been alone for more than an hour. Shaking his head in amazement, Marsh walked out past the shrubs so Annie could see him.

"In the chow hall. I should have known." She laughed, a warm sound that shimmied down his spine. "Well, there's no food in there yet, but if you'll come fire up the grill, I'll cook some hamburgers."

Marsh hesitated only a second before abandoning his plan to tour the dorms. It was dusky dark on a Thursday night, and he'd traveled many miles that day. Tomorrow would be soon enough to make inspection.

"Actually, I went in there to repair the dishwasher," he told Annie when he joined her on Hal's cedar deck.

"I know. I was just teasing," Annie said. She handed him a bag of charcoal, then disappeared into the kitchen. "Did you find out what's wrong?" she asked through the screen door. Marsh could just see her busily unloading a grocery bag.

"I did." He stacked the briquettes in the grill. "And I can't repair it."

"That's too bad." She didn't sound a bit upset.

"And neither can anyone else," Marsh added, just in case her stoicism meant she'd never believed he had the skills to do it. He searched all over the deck and finally found the charcoal lighter fluid tucked behind a clay flowerpot, then doused his carefully constructed pyramid with a generous squirt. "That old thing must be forty years old. It's rusted, worn out."

"Hmm. Well, you get to tell Hal."

"Why me?"

"Because you're in charge."

"Not by choice," he reminded her, adding, "Got a match?"

"Somewhere," she replied. "The trick is to find them..." Marsh heard the screech of a drawer, then the sounds of Annie searching through it. "Aha!"

She joined him on the deck a second later, but instead of handing him the matches, she struck one against the cast-iron grill and tossed it right onto the soaked briquettes.

Flames whooshed from the grill even as Marsh shoved her out of harm's way.

"What the hell are you trying to do?" he yelled at her.

"Start the fire, of course." Eyes wide, Annie stared at the grill, now billowing with smoke and flame. "I had no idea self-lighting briquettes would go up like that. They ought to put a warning on the bag."

Self-lighting? Marsh groaned aloud at his carelessness. "Damn, Annie. I doused them with lighter fluid."

Their gazes locked. To his amazement, she laughed heartily. "That explains it, then. Luckily, there's no harm done. At least I don't think there is." Annie picked up a strand of her coppery hair and examined it closely. "Am I singed?"

Marsh leaned closer to make inspection of her silky-looking tresses, just resisting the urge to touch. "Nope."

"Thank goodness," Annie said with a sigh. "Though that would've been the perfect excuse to cut it. Heaven knows I've been trying to get up the nerve for years—"

"You're going to cut your hair?" Marsh cringed at the very thought of someone shearing those fiery locks.

"I've been thinking about it." She seemed a bit startled by his horror. "It's so hard to comb out when it's wet."

"So let someone else do it." He touched his fingers to her hair, just as soft as he'd imagined.

"I don't have a handmaiden, Marsh," Annie told him. "Or a husband."

How about a lover? That question echoed so loudly in Marsh's head that for a moment he feared he'd really asked it. But Annie didn't blink, a sure indication he hadn't.

"Don't cut it," he therefore said. "It's your trademark. Why, every time I've thought of you over the years, I've pictured that hair." Too late, Marsh realized what he'd just admitted—something he'd never even acknowledged to himself.

"You've thought of me?" Of course she wouldn't let such a statement go unnoticed. What woman could?

"Now and then," he said, and waited for the *When?* that was sure to follow.

"I've thought of you, too," she said instead, an answer that hit him like a punch to the gut. "Lots." She touched her index finger lightly to the cleft in his chin. "It's good to have you home, Marsh."

Home? She said that word as though Timbertop belonged to her. Or maybe she figured she belonged to Timbertop, just as he did. Oddly bothered by the idea of sharing his haven with Annie, Marsh abruptly changed the subject. "Where's the rack for this thing?"

"Inside." She left him, then, to go inside. Marsh made the most of the opportunity to catch his breath, and by the time Annie returned, he had fully recovered and raised his guard again.

As a result, he kept his distance and his cool. And as a result of that, he caught her watching him on more than one occasion during their meal, her brows knitted in a slight frown.

But she asked no questions, and when they finished eating their hamburgers, she accepted his offer to help clean up the kitchen.

"Did you notice what Hal's done to the boat dock?" Annie asked sometime later as she stacked the last plate in the cupboard.

"Actually, I haven't even been out to the lake yet."

"Then let's go for a walk."

"But it's dark out," Marsh replied.

"It is not. We have another thirty minutes of daylight left."

"Fifteen, tops."

"Are you afraid of the night, Marsh McGriffey?"

"Not of the night," Marsh told her. "But I am afraid of breaking my neck trying to maneuver that path to the lake. It's a tricky walk at high noon, and you know it."

"What I know is that you could make that trek blindfolded."

"Maybe."

"Then make it now . . . with me."

"Oh, all right," he said, as curious about what Hal had done to the boat dock as he was reluctant to stroll the woods with Annie in the dark.

They said little during the walk through the trees, probably because Marsh answered Annie's questions in monosyllables until she gave up any attempt at conversation. Gradually the deep purple of the eastern sky sneaked up on the pinks and lavenders of the western. Tree frogs began to serenade. A night breeze rustled the leaves.

Annie tripped over a tree root, barely visible in the well-worn path.

"Are you okay?" Marsh growled at her, marveling that she hadn't fallen flat on her face.

"I'm fine," she snapped back, then whirled around to block his path. "Are you?"

"What do you mean?"

"I mean you're as grouchy as an old bear. What's wrong with you?"

"Simply put—I don't want to be out here."

"Out here?" Annie asked, her features a blur in the dusky dark. "Or at Timbertop? In other words, are you sorry you agreed to stay and help Hal?"

"Of course not," Marsh said, avoiding her gaze, which probed him through the gloom. "I'm glad to help Hal."

"Then what's wrong?"

"Nothing's wrong," Marsh said. "And if I'm in such a bad mood as you think I am, I apologize...okay?"

She thought about it, then shrugged. "I guess it will have to be, won't it?" That said, she headed down the path once more.

Marsh caught up with her in two strides and caught her arm at the elbow. "Annie...wait."

She did, but with obvious reluctance.

"I want to help Hal. I'm willing to stay for as long as it takes to do it."

"Willing but not eager, is that it?"

"Not eager, true, but not sorry, either. I just didn't come prepared to stay more than a couple of days. I didn't stop my mail or my newspaper. I didn't bring enough clothes. I didn't even tell my editor where I was going." He smiled at her. "So if I'm not eager, exactly, don't hold it against me. I'll get into the spirit of this thing before long . . . maybe when I see the lake."

"You think?"

"Won't know till we get there," he replied, giving her a little push in that direction. She laughed softly in response and promptly stumbled again, at which point Marsh took the lead.

The years had not altered the twists and turns of that old path, and, as predicted, he traversed the rest of it without further mishap. Annie did the same, probably because she slipped a finger through his middle back belt loop and stepped wherever he stepped.

Exactly thirty-eight minutes after they left Hal's house, they burst through the trees into the cleared area that encircled the lake. Black as midnight, smooth as glass, it lay before them, and Marsh had to grin, suddenly recalling another late visit to these very shores.

He'd been nineteen at the time and on his way to six weeks of basic training for the army. He and Hal had made this same walk, but they'd had lanterns, fishing rods and bait.

"So what do you think?" Annie asked, yanking him out of his memories.

Marsh glanced in the direction of the boat dock, about fifty feet to their left. Since they'd left the shadowy woods behind them, he could clearly see the improvements—new planks, railing, built-in benches.

"The old one finally collapsed. Hal decided to put a rail on this one so the younger kids could walk out on it."

"Good idea," Marsh commented. He reached back to loosen Annie's finger from his belt loop, then took her hand in his. Together, they walked out onto the floating dock, which dipped slightly with every step and made sunset-hued ripples in the onyx water.

At the end of the long projection, they sat. Annie on one side, Marsh on the other. Silence reigned for a moment—human silence, that is. All around them were inhuman sounds: the croaks of frogs, the chirrups of the crickets, the hum of whatever insect whizzed past.

Marsh relished each and every one of those noises and the smells, too—new wood, honeysuckle, pine.

"Nice, huh?" Annie murmured, as though reading his mind.

Marsh looked her way and smiled. "Damned nice. Timbertop will always be special to me. I had the time of my life here."

"And speaking of your life, what have you been doing for the past eighteen years, Marsh Mc-Griffey?"

"The usual stuff," he told her with a shrug. "I joined the army at nineteen. Did that for four years."

"Were you stationed stateside?"

"Nah, and I didn't want to be. I joined the military so I could see the world, and that's what I did."

"How'd you like it—the army, I mean?"

"I loved it...for the first three years. Then they put me behind a desk."

"Uh-oh," she murmured with a chuckle of sympathy. "So what did you do next?"

"I landed a job with Lady Liberty Broadcasting Company. I was their roving reporter for the prime-time news for the next seven years."

"And did a bang-up job, I might add," Annie said.

"You watched me?" Her compliment surprised him.

"Every night on Channel Twenty. You were a natural."

"Thanks," he murmured rather self-consciously.

"Such a natural," she continued, "that I wonder why you quit."

He considered that question—one he'd answered before—as though hearing it for the first time. "I was tired," he finally told her, a truth he'd never shared before. "Tired of crooked politicians, tired of foolish wars, tired of tragedy. I wanted to report something upbeat for a change. I wanted to go where I chose, when I chose." He leaned forward slightly, his elbows on his knees, and met her steady gaze. "Does any of this make sense?"

Annie nodded and then stood. Moving across the dock, she sat next to Marsh and lay an arm lightly across his shoulders in a sort of hug.

"All of it makes sense," she told him, words that somehow made everything all better and brought to mind his own comment that she had a knack for healing little hurts. "So what did you do next?"

"I dug out all the photographs I'd taken while I was in the army—I had hundreds of them—and picked out the best. Then I pounded the pavement, photos in hand, until I found a publisher willing to take a chance."

"And the rest is history," Annie interjected with a laugh. "I've seen your first book, and I have to tell you that it touched me."

Marsh said nothing, as always ill-at-ease when told how this or that photo of his "touched" someone.

"Lucky you," he murmured in a voice as cold and flat as his emotions these days. "I can't remember the last time anything or anyone touched me." At her look of concern, he laughed without humor. "Occupational hazard, I guess." He cleared his throat and abruptly changed the topic of conversation. "So, what have *you* been doing for the past eighteen years?"

"Nothing so exciting as seeing the world, I'm afraid," she told him, drawing back her arm, standing. She walked to the very end of the dock and leaned over it, staring at the inky black water. Overhead, stars now twinkled, and low on the eastern horizon, Marsh saw the uppermost curve of the rising moon, orange as a Halloween pumpkin.

"So you didn't move around as much as I did. So what?"

"Oh, but I *did* move around as much as you did—maybe even more. Why, from my ninth birthday to my eighteenth I lived in sixteen different foster homes and orphanages."

Marsh's jaw dropped. "You're lying."

"I never lie," Annie said, and he could tell she meant it.

"But you were such a cute kid and so likable..."

"Cute?" She considered that word in silence for a moment. "Maybe in a Huckleberry Finn sort of way. Likable? Never. I had a sassy mouth, a curious mind and a streak of mischief. I fought with my foster siblings. I played hooky from school. I ran away. In short, I wasn't worth the trouble, and all my foster parents—most of whom tried very hard to get along with me—eventually admitted it and gave up trying.''

Marsh couldn't believe his ears. ''What happened?''

''Lots,'' she said. ''And I'll be glad to tell you all of it . . . back at the house. These mosquitoes are eating me alive.''

Marsh, who'd just been bitten by one himself, could only agree. So the two of them made their way back through the familiar woods, Marsh in the lead and stepping with care.

Once back at the house, Annie poured them both a glass of tea, then herded Marsh to Miss Opal's parlor, which looked exactly as it had when she was alive.

After motioning Marsh to the velvet couch, Annie sat in an ornate, high-backed chair and tucked her legs up under her. He noted that she had picked up a throw pillow and now hugged it to her chest. She seemed a bit down, he thought, and wondered if his delving into her past had anything to do with it.

Nonetheless, he picked up their conversation right where they'd dropped it out in the woods. ''Now where were we. . . .'' he prompted, words that earned him a grimace from Annie.

''Looking back,'' she told him. ''And it's not a pretty picture.''

''I've seen worse.''

''I'll bet you have,'' Annie said. She sipped her tea, then plucked absently at the needlepoint design on the pillow in her arms. ''Don't get me wrong, Marsh. I'm not complaining about being shifted from home to home. Not at all. I know that I owe each and every one of those warm-hearted people who took me in a big apology, and I've managed to give it to most of them, along with the thank-you they deserve.''

Marsh chuckled. "What happened after high school?''

"College," she replied. "Courtesy of Hal and Opal.''

"He paid for your nursing degree?''

"Uh-huh.''

"I had no idea.''

"I'm not surprised. Hal helps from the heart, not for the praise of his fellow man...but you must know that. You've benefited from his generosity yourself.''

"I did indeed," Marsh said, then finished off his drink. "Tell me about your college years.''

"They were probably the happiest of my life," Annie replied. "I attended classes all morning, then worked all night as a nurse's aide.''

"When did you study?''

"In the afternoons.''

"Hmm. When did you sleep?''

"I didn't...at least not much...but I was so happy. Then I landed my first job.''

Marsh took note of the subtle change in her voice, saw her slight frown. "Where?''

"In the emergency room of Roanoke General.''

"How long did you stay there?''

"Five years.''

"And what did you like best about it?'' Marsh asked, setting down his empty glass and stretching out full length on Opal's couch, his head on the wooden armrest.

"The exit. And my favorite moment was when I walked out that door and drove away for good. I was sick of stabbings, muggings and rapes. I missed small-town living. I missed Timbertop. I missed Hal."

Marsh said nothing in response. Instead he silently marveled at her tale. He, himself, had never missed anything—not even Hal, the only father he'd ever know. Sure, they'd kept in touch through the years, but not because Marsh couldn't get along without Hal.

No, siree. And now, for the very first time, Marsh's lack of emotion worried him some. Heretofore proud of his Gypsy life-style and the fact that he needed no human contact to obtain peace of mind and happiness, Marsh actually found himself reassessing his dispassion.

That disconcerted him a bit, and because it did, he once again changed the subject rather abruptly.

"So what are your goals, Annie? Are you going to stay buried up here at Timbertop forever? You know you could make better money somewhere else."

"Money isn't everything," she quoted to him, and then smiled.

"But surely you want more out of life than the thrill of bandaging minor cuts and bruises or dabbing cal-amine lotion on a poison-ivy rash."

"I have goals," she said, "just like any other twenty-seven-year-old woman. I want to marry. I want kids."

"The family you never had?"

She nodded, then got up to stuff her pillow behind Marsh's head. "What about you? What are your goals?"

Marsh stared at the ceiling, trying to decide. "Immediate? Finishing this book."

"And long range?" She walked to a whatnot shelf and began to inspect what she found on it.

"I want to travel some more—but this time to where I *want* to go."

"And will you be traveling alone? Or are a wife and children also in your plans?"

"No wife. No children," Marsh told her without hesitation. "I fly solo."

"Oh?" Her question invited him to expand, to explain. But he didn't oblige. Marsh didn't set as much stock in family ties as she did, probably because of his experience with them.

He looked at his watch. "It's getting late." He sat up, swung his feet to the floor and feigned a yawn. "I'm bushed."

Standing, he walked to the door of the parlor, where Annie quickly joined him. "Me, too, and there's so much to do tomorrow." She grinned. "Since you're a guest, you can have first dibs on the shower."

"I'm no more a guest than you," Marsh retorted, nudging her out into the hall.

"No matter. You can still be first, but wait until I get some clean towels, okay? They're all folded, but still laying on the dryer."

"Why don't I just use this shower down here?" Marsh asked. "That way no one has to wait."

"Not enough water pressure," Annie informed him.

"But I repaired the pump, remember?"

Annie laughed. "Actually, I'd forgotten. What a luxury. I'll be right back with the towels." That said, she headed toward the basement steps that led, Marsh knew, to the laundry room.

He walked to the bathroom and stuck his hand inside the door, groping for the wall switch to turn on the light. But when he flipped it, the bulb flashed eerily and popped.

"Damn!" Marsh muttered. Turning, he ran smack into Annie, back from the basement with an armload of towels, and nearly knocked her to the floor.

Marsh cursed again, but Annie just giggled and ordered him to pick up the now scattered towels while she searched for a new bulb. Within minutes, bright light illuminated the tiny bath, and he stashed the towels in the linen closet. Shortly after that, Marsh stood under the stinging spray, congratulating himself on the wonderful repair job he'd done on the pump.

He could tell the exact moment Annie turned on the upstairs shower, since the force of the water lessened considerably. But since he was finished by then, it didn't matter. Making short work of slipping into the clean sweatpants retrieved earlier from his bag, Marsh took the stairs two at a time and walked into his bedroom.

From the bathroom next door, he heard the sounds of Annie in the shower—the swish of the plastic curtain, the splash of the water against the porcelain tub.

Immediately his head filled with a vision of Annie standing under the hot spray, her skin glowing pink. Never mind that he'd never seen her au naturel, he could still imagine how she'd look, and for just one second indulged himself in his fantasy.

"Argh!"

That cry came from the bath, and Marsh leapt to his feet. He heard no other sound, not even running water; then the door flew open and Annie burst through it—her hair a halo of shampoo bubbles, her body encased in an oversized terry robe, her feet dripping sudsy water on the wooden floor.

"Marsh!"

"I'm right here," he calmly replied, not a bit surprised she hadn't seen him. How could she with her eyes squinched so tightly shut?

"What happened to the water?"

So much for a job well done. It was all Marsh could do not to laugh at her predicament. "You don't have water?"

"I don't." She wiped her eyes with the sleeve of her robe, then opened them very slowly, as though testing to see if she'd removed all the soap. "Nor do I have a towel."

"I thought you got them. . . ."

"I did. Where are they?"

"In the linen closet," he told her, chuckling when he added, "Downstairs."

"Oh, for—" She threw her hands up in agitation, a move that launched a handful of soap bubbles into the air.

That did it, of course. Marsh howled with laughter.

Annie screeched her outrage and lunged for him, actually landing a couple of playful punches to his bare midsection before he could capture her hands and pin them to his chest.

Aware of her state of temper, he honestly tried to curb his mirth. But she was such a sight in that monstrous robe, with those soapsuds running down her face...

Only when Annie kicked him in the shin with her bare foot did Marsh acknowledge that things had gone too far. In one swift move, he engulfed his irate housemate full in his arms and hefted her up to where she was nose-to-nose with him. Eyes wide, her mouth an O of surprise, she stopped struggling.

"I'll get the damn towels," he promised.

And then, giving in to the proximity of those pretty, pursed lips and a need he could never explain, Marsh kissed her.

Chapter Three

The moment Marsh's lips touched Annie's, she tensed. Shock shimmied up her spine to be followed by shivers of . . . what?

Desire?

Undoubtedly, Annie realized as she threw her arms around his neck and returned the kiss full measure. In an instant, nothing else mattered but that delicious contact. Annie's head swam; her knees buckled. Her bare breasts brushed Marsh's bare chest. . . .

Gasping in realization, Annie abruptly released him and tore herself away. She clutched the traitorous, gaping robe with both hands and then, highly conscious of Marsh's gasping for breath, whirled and dashed back into the bathroom, slamming and locking the door behind her.

There she did a little gasping of her own.

"Oh, my goodness—" pant, pant "—Oh, my goodness."

Annie paced as she panted, as startled as she was intrigued that her hero had fallen from his pedestal... right into her arms.

"Annie?" Marsh knocked on the door. "Are you okay?"

"Fine," she managed to croak, blushing anew.

"Stay put. I'm going to go outside and work on the pump again."

Annie nodded but, still breathless, couldn't verbalize her reply this time.

"Did you hear me?"

"I... heard."

Dead silence greeted her halting reply. Then, "Are you sure you're okay?" His voice sounded closer now, as though his face were pressed against the wooden barrier that separated them.

At once Annie's heart began to hammer and she felt a sort of ache deep inside. "I tell you I'm fine. Now would you please hurry with that pump? I've got to get this soap out of my hair."

He laughed then, a sound that did wonders to bring Annie back to earth. With a shake of her head to further clear it, she went to work, rewrapping the oversized robe and securing it with the sash. Then she sat on the side of the antique tub and waited, her thoughts on anything and everything but what had just transpired between her and Marsh.

For ten minutes she sat that way—numb—then Marsh knocked on the bathroom door again.

"Annie?"

Annie leapt to her feet and opened the door a crack. "Is it fixed already?"

"Nah." Marsh looked as disgusted as he sounded. "I can't repair it this time." He held up a plastic bucket. "Here's the primer water. Do what you can."

Dubiously Annie eyed the scant five gallons of liquid. Was she supposed to rinse her whole body and a head full of hair with that?

"Want me to heat it?"

"No," Annie grumbled, reaching through the door for the bucket and for the towel he held in his other hand.

"I really don't mind."

"No." Firmly, she closed the door again. Then she stepped out of the robe and into the tub where she made short work of rinsing off what soap the terry cloth of her robe had not already absorbed from her body.

That accomplished, Annie used the last two gallons to rinse her hair. Though she usually tamed her riotous mane with a conditioner, tonight she could not afford the luxury and so contented herself with removing all traces of shampoo.

She paid dearly for that omission moments later, of course, when she tried to comb out her tangled curls.

"Ouch!" Annie exclaimed after several minutes of painful tugging on a particularly stubborn knot of hair. By now in a temper, she gave the hair pick a fling into the bathtub.

"What's going on in there?" It was Marsh, and from the sound of things he was right outside the bathroom door again.

In no mood to explain, Annie ignored him and picked up a hairbrush. But he wasn't to be ignored—a fact made clear when he knocked on the door and then rattled the knob.

"Annie?"

With a snort of impatience, she flung open the door. "What?"

"Are you okay?"

"I already told you that I am," she snapped at him, and then swiped at her hair with the brush.

With solemn eyes, he assessed her. Then he reached out and took the brush. "I'll be your handmaiden tonight," he said with a chuckle, ridiculously solemn words that reminded her of their earlier conversation.

He readily volunteered to play handmaiden—more readily than he would ever offer to be anyone's husband, she suspected. That realization troubled Annie. Why, she couldn't imagine. Heaven knew he didn't impact on her own dreams and goals. Marsh was nothing to her but a hero turned friend.

And their kiss . . . Well, it was a nothing, too.

"All right, handmaiden," she replied. "See what you can do with this mess." She turned to allow him access to the damp hair tumbling over her shoulders and down her back.

"Let's sit," he answered, and led the way to his bed. High, wide and inviting, it dominated the room, and Annie felt a shiver of unease she could not explain.

Nonetheless, she perched on one edge of the deep blue comforter and turned slightly so Marsh could sit close behind her. Once settled, he began to gently untangle her hair with the brush.

"You're very good at this," Annie commented to break the silence. Her words sounded strangely husky. "Ever been anyone else's handmaiden?"

"Actually, now that I think about it, valet would be a more appropriate term," Marsh replied. "And to answer your question, no, though I might've if I'd known how much fun it could be."

Fun? Try stimulating, and his tender ministrations soon took their toll on Annie. Every nerve ending in her body stood up and begged for Marsh's attention. She heard herself sigh—a foolish female sound—and swayed back against him, overcome with a sudden need to get closer.

Marsh chuckled in response, a sound that jerked Annie right back to reality. Mortified, she tried to sit up straight again, but he wrapped his arms around her midriff, preventing escape.

"Tired?" he whispered into the top of her head.

"Exhausted," she lied, grateful he'd given her an excuse for her behavior. Since her wits had long since vanished, she could never have come up with one of her own.

"Then it's off to bed with you, young lady," Marsh responded, his voice light and teasing. He stood, and, to Annie's astonishment, scooped her up in his arms.

"What are you doing?" she blurted as he walked through the bathroom into her quarters and deposited her on her bed.

"Good night, Annie," Marsh said, handing her the hairbrush.

"Good night," she murmured as he retreated, turning off the bathroom light as he passed through. Since he did not shut either connecting door, she heard every move he made in preparation for retiring and then the squeak of the bed when he climbed into it and turned out his light.

Her own bed felt quite cold and oddly empty. And the ache deep inside became a need that shocked and bewildered her.

Annie's hand shook when she reached to turn off her lamp. In the dark, she skinnied out of her robe and into a soft satin gown. Then she crawled between crisp cotton sheets and turned to face her open window.

Thanks to the attic fan, a cool breeze blew in, but did not affect her overheated libido. At once restless, Annie threw back the sheet and slipped out of the bed to walk over to the window. She sat on the sill so she could look out, but really saw nothing, even though the full moon illuminated the earth and sky.

Thoughts spun in her head. New feelings knotted in the pit of her stomach. But try as she might, Annie could not come to any conclusion about Marsh or the kiss they had shared.

Frustrated, she gave up second-guessing his motives. Instead she concentrated on her own.

She'd kissed the man back. There was no denying that.

She'd enjoyed doing it, too.

So what's wrong with that? Annie asked herself. It wasn't as though she were sweet sixteen and inexperienced in that department. She'd actually been kissed a lot in her life . . . usually by a date with high hopes. Annie had always disappointed those dates and with no regret on her part—an indication, she believed, that she hadn't as yet met her love match. Never had any man's kiss disturbed her, tempted her.

Never until now...and that, of course, explained her current dilemma. She found that she wanted more from this man—from Marsh—than mere kisses. She found she wanted to...explore their physical differences.

Did her wanton reaction mean Marsh might be her long-awaited love match? Annie scoffed at the mere idea. Surely Mother Nature—a woman—would not play so dirty a trick on one of her own kind. Surely Annie's love match would not be a man who scorned marriage, an institution she held so dear.

True, Marsh always claimed a special place in her heart. But so did all the other people who'd been kind to her through the years. Annie owed them much and loved them all.

And that, of course, explained everything. Her feelings for Marsh—though platonic—were strong, and she'd simply misread them.

As for this ache so deep inside... Perhaps it was just a woman thing—something any female experienced when held by a man so virile as Marsh. None of her dates compared, so of course she hadn't reacted this way before.

Yeah, that was it.

Annie sighed with relief and deliberately turned her thoughts to other things. In seconds, her head filled with new images—images of all that had to be done before Timbertop opened its gates to campers. At once she felt overwhelmed by the enormity of her task, and fatigue set in again.

With another sigh, this one of weariness, Annie returned to her bed. And when she closed her eyes this time, she slept.

* * *

Marsh rose before dawn the next morning after a sleepless night haunted by hot kisses and self-recrimination. He dressed quickly in a pair of much-worn camouflage pants and a matching T-shirt. Both comfortable, if a little out of place here at Timbertop, they'd served him well last year while working on his wildlife book.

After slipping downstairs without making a sound, he then headed right outside. There, Marsh walked the length and breadth of Timbertop with purposeful strides, noting this and that rotting timber, leaky pipe and sagging roof.

Dismay stole the pleasure from his tour, and not even the discovery of two freshly scrubbed and waiting dormitories could restore it. What memories those old dorms held for him—happy memories of midnight whispers, ghost stories, never-ending songs.

But even those living quarters needed work, so much, in fact, that dismay settled over Marsh like a thick wool blanket.

Why had Hal neglected the place? he naturally wondered. Too much expense? Too little help?

Ennui?

No, not ennui. Never that. Hal loved Timbertop too much. The camp was his life and if it now fell apart, there was a good reason. Marsh simply had to figure out what that reason was.

That in mind, he headed for the woods that covered most of the acres that were Timbertop. A stiff breeze rustled the treetops overhead. Marsh spied a dogwood and paused beside it, the artist in him appreciating the sharp contrast of delicate white blossom to bare branch.

A bee buzzed noisily close, but Marsh never even blinked. At one with nature now, he had nothing to fear, and he breathed in the scent of the flowers that had lured the bee.

Heaven, he thought, smiling his satisfaction. Pure heaven. A scent like no other, one that should be bottled and saved for use in the dead of winter. A certain pick-me-up...

Marsh laughed aloud at his foolishness and trudged on a few yards, pausing next before an ancient sweetgum tree he knew well. Oozing from a scrape in the bark, he spied crystallized sap. With a grin, Marsh dug his pocketknife out of his pants, scraped the crystals off the tree and popped them into his mouth.

This gum, though not exactly sweet, didn't taste half bad, and Marsh began to chew. He then closed his eyes and relaxed against the trunk of the tree for several long moments, lost in old pleasures, before moving on to another familiar tree, this one an oak.

Adjacent to a clear-running stream, it had provided him with many an hour of fun, high atop its sturdy branches. How many times had he climbed that tree and hid there in the leaves, thinking his way through a problem?

Marsh didn't know and didn't wonder long. Instead, he reached up to a low-lying limb and tested its strength. Still sturdy, he decided, impulsively swinging his legs up to gain a foothold on the gnarled bark. With the swiftness of a well-learned skill, Marsh climbed to sit high in its swaying branches.

There he sat for a while, watching the sunrise in the east, enjoying the soothing sway of the branches in the breeze. Nearby, a mockingbird greeted the morning.

Below, a squirrel, not fooled by the color of Marsh's clothing, scolded and fussed. As oblivious to them as to the passing of time, Marsh never heard anything.

Until his watched beeped the hour.

Absently Marsh glanced down at it. What he saw shocked him so badly that he nearly fell from his perch.

"Damn!" There was much to be done today. He had no time for daydreaming.

Quickly, Marsh grabbed the nearest branch and maneuvered himself into position for a hasty descent. But he managed only one small step before he heard singing—Annie-type singing—and quite close. His heart in his throat, Marsh froze and turned to peer down over his shoulder at the path below, just visible through a canopy of leaves.

It was Annie, carrying some sort of bundle. Marsh almost hailed her, then caught himself before she could see that he'd climbed that old tree just like some little kid. Grateful for the breeze and rustling leaves that disguised his movements, he waited for her to walk on up the path.

But she didn't, and since his arms now ached with his weight, Marsh watched until she stopped to examine a dew-burnished spider web, then levered himself ever so carefully back up to his old perch, from where he watched to see what she would do next.

Abandoning the sparkling web, she tossed her bundle down right at the foot of his tree. Annie then stepped over to the creek, slipped out of one of her sandals and tested the water with a toe.

Marsh frowned. Surely she wasn't going to swim in that icy water....

As though in answer to his unspoken question, Annie slipped out of her other sandal, then grabbed her T-shirt by the hem. Before Marsh could react, she pulled it right over her head, and before he recovered from that shocker, she stepped out of her denim cutoffs.

Immediately, Marsh abandoned any half-formed notions of revealing his presence. How could he embarrass her—and himself—in that way?

With determination he didn't know he possessed, Marsh looked up and away from the nymph below. And it was only when he heard a splash and a squeal that he risked a peek at her.

Dressed only in brief panties and a lacy bra, Annie now stood knee-deep in water that had to be ice cold. She laughed—an enchanting sound—and Marsh instantly guessed that she'd done this before.

Since her lingerie revealed no more than a French bikini, Marsh did not look away again, but watched her twist her hair into a knot up off her neck and then wet down her skin with the clear creek water, undoubtedly removing any soap she might have missed last night.

Her skin glistened golden brown in the morning sun, and he was struck by her grace and beauty. No child, this, he realized, experiencing a rush of relief that effectively explained his guilt about last night's kiss.

Despite yesterday's admission that Annie was "all grown up" and even despite his glimpse of her womanly silhouette shortly after, Marsh still thought of her as the scrawny copper-top who'd tagged along all those years ago. For that reason, he could not condone his physical response to her or his initiation of their kiss.

But she wasn't a child at all, he assured himself. She was a woman—fully grown, single, desirable. And, full-grown, single, desirous male that Marsh was, he could no more control his attraction to her than he could his body's traitorous reaction.

So simple.

So damn complicated.

At that moment Annie stepped from the creek and, to Marsh's dismay, stretched out on a beach towel she'd spread atop the velvety moss. Clearly she intended to let the sun dry her skin and her undies. And who could blame her? Certainly not the mixed-up fool trapped high above.

So he sat in silence, marveling that she did not see him up there in the branches . . . until he remembered what he wore: camouflage.

No wonder.

Finally—an eternity later—she sat up and stretched. Then she stood, dressed, snatched up her towel and headed back through the woods, once again singing as she ducked low-lying branches and stepped over fallen logs.

Marsh waited until she disappeared from view before making a move. Then, groaning with agony, he descended limb by limb, stiff muscles protesting their abuse, only to hobble back to camp much like a tenderfoot in too tight cowboy boots.

The moment Marsh stepped into the clearing of the camp proper, he spied Annie through the kitchen window. Since he didn't want her to wonder where he'd been, he waited until she moved out of sight before slipping to the back door.

There, he stopped long enough to spit out the sweet gum before pulling back the screen door and walking inside.

Annie whirled around when he did, clearly startled. "My goodness," she exclaimed, eyes wide. "Are you up already?"

In more ways than you'll ever know, Marsh silently replied. Aloud he simply murmured, "Hours ago. I've been walking around, checking out my old haunts."

"Yeah?" She seemed a little disconcerted. "What haunts?"

"Oh…the dorms, the recreation hall, the trails…"

"You went in the woods?"

"Just a little ways." Marsh walked over to the stove, on which sat a blackened cast-iron skillet filled with sizzling bacon. "Man, oh, man, does this ever smell good."

Annie said nothing for a moment, all the while eyeing him; then she joined him at the stove. "Thanks. How many eggs can you eat?"

"Three, over easy," Marsh replied without hesitation, grateful he'd diverted her from this morning's activities.

"Coming up. You've got just enough time to wash." She shooed him away, just like Opal used to do. Laughing, Marsh turned toward the door that led to the hall.

"What have you got all over your back?"

Annie's question halted Marsh, and not quite sure what to expect, he tugged at his shirt and tried to peer over his shoulder. "Where?"

"Here." She plucked at the back of his shirt. "It's tree bark and it's sticky."

"Yeah?" He tried to sound surprised even though he immediately guessed what that "sticky" was—sweetgum sap. "Must have gotten into something in the woods. I'll change shirts when I wash up." That said, Marsh escaped upstairs to his room, where he made short work of changing.

When he returned to the kitchen, he found Annie setting the table and quickly moved to help her. In seconds, they both sat and began to eat.

"What did you think of Timbertop, Marsh?" Annie tore off a corner of buttery toast and nibbled on it, her steady gaze on her breakfast companion.

"I think it's falling apart, and I want to know why."

"I knew you were going to say that," Annie replied with a sigh. "I was so shocked when I arrived earlier this week . . . but I just didn't know how to broach the subject to Hal without hurting his feelings. I'm not very tactful as a rule."

"I think we need to make a list of all that must be done, prioritize it and then confront him. He's no fool, Annie. He's bound to know the place is falling apart."

"Of course, he does," Annie replied. "That's why we climbed up on the roof earlier this week—to try to stop the leaks."

"Which reminds me . . . there's a storm front headed our way. According to the weatherman, it'll be here by the first of next week. How bad are these leaks?"

"Bad."

"And when's the roofer coming?"

"As soon as he finishes the job he's on now. He said it might be the first of next week."

"Then I'd better see about the leak myself."

Annie frowned. "Do you have to? That roof has such a steep pitch..."

"I can do it," Marsh replied, and took a last sip of his coffee. He then stood to gather up his dirty dishes.

"I'll take care of these," Annie told him. "You go get the shingles. They're in the shed. The ladder is, too, but don't climb until I get out there to hold it, okay?"

"Relax," Marsh told her. "Unlike Hal, I'm young and agile. I won't fall."

"Be that as it may, I want you to wait." Annie's bossy tone and judgmental glare reminded Marsh of his grandmother—a woman he hadn't thought of in years and didn't want to remember now. Instantly his mood took a turn for the worse.

"Okay, okay." Turning, Marsh left the kitchen and headed to the old storage shed a few yards from the back of the house. The door creaked as he opened it, a familiar sound that brought back memories. He peered inside and easily found the stack of shingles. Next to them lay the ladder, and next to it were the fishing poles.

Marsh eyed those poles for a full minute, sorely tempted to put Hal's leaky old roof on hold while he paid the lake a little visit. He didn't give in to temptation, of course, and soon stood next to the house, positioning the ladder so he could climb it.

When he finished, he glanced around for Annie, who was nowhere in sight, then put a foot on the bottom rung of the ladder to make sure it was securely set.

"Marsh, don't!" It was Annie, bursting out the back door. In seconds she stood beside him, out of breath and clearly upset. "I knew you wouldn't wait."

"I was only testing the damn thing," Marsh retorted, curtly adding, "Would you just cool it?"

Annie caught her breath. Bright crimson stained her cheeks. "Well, excuse me for caring," she exclaimed, then whirled as though to leave him and his ladder alone.

"Wait!" In a heartbeat, Marsh caught her by the arm and turned her to face him. This wasn't his grandmother, this was Annie. She did not want to change him. She wasn't afraid he would embarrass her. And she didn't deserve his bad temper. "I-I'm sorry. I'm not used to having someone look after me."

"I just don't want you to get hurt, too," Annie told him.

"Running this place alone would be a bummer, wouldn't it?" he muttered with a dry laugh, words he regretted instantly.

Annie flinched as though that low blow were physical instead of verbal. "That's a hell of a thing to say."

"Yeah," Marsh agreed with some embarrassment. "And I really don't know why I said it."

"Well, I do." Annie crossed her arms over her chest and glared up at him. "You've been alone so long that you don't know how to act around other people—especially other people who care about you."

"Are you saying I'm antisocial?" Marsh asked, oddly insulted.

"Not antisocial, exactly. More . . . scared."

Marsh snorted at that. "Of what, for crying out loud?"

"Of being human. Of maybe caring back. And so you growl, hoping the sound will scare everyone away."

"My, my, aren't you the clever one?" Marsh murmured with sarcasm to hide his discomfort at the truth of her words.

"Not so clever," she softly replied. "But very concerned."

"Don't be," he told her. "I'm not worth it."

"Oh, but you are." Annie reached up to trace his jawline with her fingertips. "When I think what you did for me that summer so long ago..."

"Annie."

"Why, if you hadn't taken me fishing, there's no telling what mischief I'd have gotten into..."

"An-nie."

"And you taught me so much, too—about line, about baits, about hooks..."

"Annie!"

She blinked in surprise. "What?"

"I'm glad I made a difference in your life," Marsh told her. "And just for the record, you made a difference in mine, too. As for my avoiding people...maybe you're right. I don't know. I do know that if we don't get busy on this roof, we won't finish it before it's time to go see Hal."

"Oh, my gosh, the roof. I'd forgotten." She gave him a sheepish smile. "Sometimes I get carried away..."

Marsh shrugged in reply and stepped up to the ladder, glad their awkward moment had passed. But just as he placed his foot on the bottom rung, Annie caught his arm.

"I'd better come along. I know right where the leaks are."

"Then you go first," Marsh replied, moving back. Annie slipped in front of him and began to climb the ladder. The moment she reached eye level, Marsh yanked on the hem of her peach-colored shirt, a movement that halted her ascent and prompted her to peer over her shoulder at him.

At once unsure of himself, Marsh hesitated, then blundered on. "I-I just wanted to thank you for not being frightened of my growl."

Instead of replying, Annie turned all the way around on the ladder to face Marsh. Grabbing a handful of his shirtfront, she tugged him forward a stumbling step so she could frame his face in her hands.

"You're very welcome," she said with utter sincerity before placing a chaste kiss on the tip of his nose. Releasing him, she turned back around, or tried to. Marsh quickly grabbed the rails on either side, pinning her where she stood.

"I, um, also want to thank you for worrying about my falling off the roof."

Annie grinned. "But don't do it again?"

"Not out loud, anyway," Marsh replied.

Annie laughed at that. "You win. My lips are sealed." She placed her finger on those lips, an action that reminded Marsh how tasty they were. Instantly he considered savoring them again.

But it was too late. Annie, all business once more, had already turned and now ascended the ladder.

Marsh waited until she sat on the roof before joining her, shingles in tow. With Annie in the lead, they half walked, half crawled over the steep incline to the area in need of attention. Marsh marveled that there weren't other leaks—the entire roof was a mess—and vowed to check the attic to be sure.

"Here's where we were when Hal slipped," Annie said, pointing to an area of shingle obviously newer than the rest. "You can see we didn't get much done."

Marsh could see that and busied himself with placing the shingles and then securing them with the roof tacks Annie handed him. It wasn't a beautiful job, he knew, but it would do until they hired a professional.

"Thanks, Marsh," Annie said when he finished hammering the last nail. "Hal will be so relieved when we tell him."

Marsh nodded his agreement and stood, anxious to relieve leg muscles that had seen too much abuse that day. Instantly one of those muscles knotted in a humdinger of a charley horse so painful that he lost his footing, sat down hard and began a steady slide toward the edge of the roof.

Annie screamed her terror even as Marsh dug his heels into the weather-smoothed shingles. He managed to stop several inches from real danger, but not before his red-haired companion burst into tears.

Marsh immediately crawled back up to where she sat, her face hidden in her hands.

"Annie, Annie," he said, taking her hands in his and pulling them away from her face. "I'm all right."

"Oh, thank God," she breathed, throwing her arms around his neck in a choking hug.

The depth of her relief astounded Marsh. It seemed that Annie really did care, and only belatedly did he comprehend the full impact of a woman's caring.

It was different from Hal's caring. He and Marsh understood one another and made no demands. But with Annie's caring came responsibility. Though no more than friends with her, Marsh had somehow lost his freedom. And even as he mourned that loss, a secret part of him rejoiced in it.

Chapter Four

"We'll take care of everything," Annie said into the telephone receiver barely an hour later. Seated at Opal's rolltop desk, she tapped her pencil on the smooth oak finish.

"Thanks, honey." Hal's voice sounded oddly strained. A bad connection? Or was he ill?

"Are you feeling okay, Pops?"

"Fine, just fine," he assured her.

"Then we'll see you later," Annie promised, silently vowing to verify the state of his health for herself when she and Marsh visited him after lunch.

Just as she hung up the phone, Marsh poked his head through the door.

"I'm going out to the dorms to air the mattresses," he told her, words Annie barely registered. Having just received Hal's permission to buy a new dishwasher and well pump, she now wondered who to call for quotes. "Annie?"

Annie stared blankly at her housemate for a full second before she realized he expected an answer. Since she hadn't really heard what he'd said, she could only guess he'd shared his plans for the rest of the morning. "Um . . . have fun?"

Marsh grinned. "Right," he murmured before leaving. Annie heard him chuckling all the way down the hall, a sure sign she'd missed something. But, a woman with a mission, she didn't wonder long what it could be. Instead, she got busy, and in less than an hour, she'd compiled a list of the best brands and lowest prices available in the immediate area.

When Annie finally rose from the desk around ten o'clock, the results of her inquiries in hand, she headed straight for the kitchen in search of Marsh so she could share what she knew.

He wasn't there, of course, and Annie had no idea where to find him until a movement outside caught her eye through the window. Turning, she saw Marsh right across the yard, pruning a tree limb that compromised the path.

Smiling to herself, Annie watched him as he worked. She noted that he hadn't been idle the past hour, either. A row of mattresses, set on end and leaning against the outside of the dormitory walls, soaked in the sun's rays.

Other evidences of his labors were visible, too—a pile of split logs for the campfire, neatly trimmed hedges, a freshly painted sign for the hobby hut where the children did their arts and crafts. Annie marveled that Marsh had accomplished so much in so short a time. Clearly he would be good for Timbertop. The camp needed his touch.

And what about Annie? she found herself wondering. Did she need his touch, too?

"Hmm." Her gaze settled on Marsh's very capable hands, and she speculated as to how gentle they could be.

Disconcerted by the visions naturally following that thought, she shifted her gaze from Marsh's hands to the rest of him. Oblivious to her attention, he stretched to reach a dead limb and lower it to where he could use Hal's old bow saw. His shirt clung to his sweat-dampened back. His biceps bulged. His jeans hugged his muscled backside and long legs.

Annie's heart *kerthunked* in her chest, then pounded like a tom-tom. She laughed in disbelief at her totally female response to him, as amused as she was amazed by it. How very odd that Marsh—long-time hero, newfound friend—could evoke such a reaction. She hadn't counted on this when begging him to stay at Timbertop and couldn't really understand the reason for it.

Probably has something to do with that darned kiss, she decided after a moment's consideration. Marsh had surely caught her off guard last night...titillated and teased...awakened long-dormant desires.

The bad part was that he probably hadn't even meant to do it. She'd been half dressed at the time, after all. He was only human and surely as curious about her as she was about him. Besides, he hadn't said or done anything since to make Annie think he harbored any lustful ambitions.

So forget it.

Easily said, but done with difficulty, Annie realized... especially when part of her couldn't help but wonder if more than curiosity was to blame.

Maybe Marsh did desire her. Maybe he'd taken one look at the grown-up Annie Winslow and now burned with the need to take her.... Was that so very impossible?

Annie nearly choked at the mere idea and had to laugh.

Yes, it was impossible. And if she didn't stop thinking about it, she'd find herself feeling awkward and embarrassed next time she faced him.

So forget it, she instructed herself again, and then, oddly depressed, turned her thoughts to other things.

They drove to the hospital just after lunch and found Hal in seemingly good spirits, though Annie thought he looked a bit sad around the eyes. He told them his knee surgery had been tentatively scheduled for Monday morning—good news to his way of thinking.

Marsh, seated near the head of the bed in a rather utilitarian-looking chair, chose that moment to announce his intention to stay at Timbertop for as long as needed, words that put a big smile on Hal's face and an honest-to-goodness sparkle in his eye.

"Thanks, son," Hal told him, reaching out to pat his arm. "With you in charge, I won't have to worry about a thing." Belatedly, he glanced at Annie, who was busy watering one of the three pots of flowers that now adorned the windowsill—gifts from friends. "Not that I didn't think you could manage the place. It's just that..."

"I know, I know," she assured that dear old man, glad to witness this tangible lift of his spirits. "Marsh has already warned me how hectic Timbertop can be."

Hal laughed. "And he should know. Why, I remember the time—"

"Pops?" Marsh said that word as though he always had, but Annie knew he'd picked it up from her.

Hal paused in his storytelling, clearly a bit surprised to be interrupted. Or maybe he, too, had noticed the new form of address. "Yes?"

"There's something I need to talk to you about before you tell your tale. Something important. I, um, inspected the camp today and I—rather, we..." Marsh glanced uncertainly at Annie.

"The place is falling apart," she said in her usual forthright way.

Marsh glared at her. "What she means is, we're a bit concerned about the roofs on the dorms and the plumbing, among other things."

Hal considered that news in silence, then nodded. "I suspect you two are right to be worried. I know I've let things go a bit since Opal passed on." He said nothing else for a moment, then sighed—a melancholy sound that seemed to say his newfound high spirits had taken a nosedive. At once Annie wished she'd worded her opinion of Timbertop a bit more tactfully.

Apparently Marsh wished she had, too. He shot her a look of censure before turning his attention to Hal. "I was wondering if you'd mind if I spruced up the place a bit while I'm here," he said. "There's a lot I could do—"

"A lot we could do," Annie corrected. "And what we can't, we'll hire done. Why, you won't recognize Timbertop when you get out of here." She spoke the words lightly, trying to coax a smile. She was not prepared for Hal's soulful sigh.

"Opal would be upset with me if she could see the place. She was the practical one, you know—always telling me what needed doing. Kept the books, too."

"And speaking of those books," Annie gently interjected to end his needless guilt trip. "I did buy a well pump and a dishwasher, both of which are going to be delivered this afternoon. How do you want me to pay for them?"

"The checks are in Opal's desk, top right drawer, I think. Why don't you bring some in tomorrow when you come? I'll take care of everything then."

"All right. Now I want to hear that story of yours—the one you were going to tell us a minute ago."

Instantly the sparkle returned to Hal's eyes, and he chuckled. "It happened the first summer Marsh came to Timbertop as a camper. He was just a little thing, probably around . . . how old were you, son?"

"Six."

"You started camping that young?" Annie couldn't believe any mother would let her son leave home at such an early age.

Marsh nodded briefly in reply, but never took his gaze off Hal, a sure sign he'd rather hear the story than answer any questions about his childhood. Annie accepted that and held her tongue, but she listened closely to Hal's story, hoping to gain insight into the child who'd become Marsh McGriffey.

What she heard broke her heart, for Hal's words painted a picture of a lonely little boy. Young, shy, scared, he'd stepped from a world where children were neither seen nor heard into one where they sang at the dinner table, skipped an occasional bath and even stayed up late without fear of censure.

Not that Hal made an issue of the contrasts. They were just minor details in his story. So was Marsh's hiding in his bunk until Hal convinced him to join in the fun, and his subsequent transformation into a bundle of curiosity who never really mingled with the other campers, but who still had the time of his life.

That hyperactivity, of course, was the real point of Hal's story. It seemed a lot of children were as wild as Alice's March Hare when they first arrived at camp...especially the city kids. And while Annie laughed aloud at their antics, she couldn't help but wish Hal would share the rest of Marsh's story.

The two men spent the next hour exchanging camp memories, each more outrageous than the last. Annie, who suspected their tales had grown rather tall in the telling, didn't chide them. Instead she relished Hal's bright smile and the sound of his laughter, which was, after all, the best medicine in the world.

Too soon, Annie had to remind Marsh of the time. Standing, they said their goodbyes to Hal, who clung to Annie with one hand and reached for Marsh with the other. That move clearly embarrassed the loner, but he didn't pull away.

Noting that Hal's eyes now brimmed with tears, Annie squeezed his hand. "What's wrong, honey?"

"I'm a lot of trouble..."

"Not half as much as we've been to you," Annie retorted, hoping to lighten the mood.

But Hal, who clearly had something on his mind, didn't smile back. "I—I have a favor to ask. I know I have no right, but—"

"Ask your favor, Pops," Marsh interjected, his voice as gentle as Annie had ever heard it.

Hal, suddenly looking every one of his seventy-six years, nodded solemnly. "I want you two to promise that you'll carry on the tradition of Timbertop if something happens to me."

"I'll do my very best," Annie replied, words spoken easily since they came from the heart. She then turned her attention to Marsh, as anxious as Hal must be to hear his reply.

"What do you mean, if something happens to you?" Marsh roared, an answer that cleverly startled the old man. "You're in better shape than I am, except for that bum knee."

Hal's eyes rounded. "You think so?"

"I do, and I don't want to hear any more foolishness about anything happening. Hell, Pops, I'll give you ten-to-one odds you'll be hiking to Red Ridge before the summer's over."

Hal laughed then, and, beaming, related a memory of one of those traditional hikes to Red Ridge, a sure indication he'd forgotten dying—at least for the moment.

Annie didn't forget, though, and verbalized her concerns the moment she and Marsh began the drive back to camp.

"Do you think he's going to be all right?" she asked.

Marsh took his eyes off the highway just long enough to read her expression. "You're the nurse, Annie. You tell me."

She sighed the truth of that. "I'm not talking about the surgery. It's really rather routine these days."

"Even on a seventy-year-old?"

"Six. He's seventy-six, and, yes, I honestly believe he'll come through the surgery just fine. Now his age could be a factor in his rehabilitation, but he's so active, I'm not really worried about that, either."

"So what's on your mind?" Marsh asked after another quick glance her way.

"Hal's mental well-being," Annie admitted. "He seemed awfully depressed when we got there."

"But not when we left," Marsh reminded her.

"True..." She uttered the word somewhat hesitantly.

Marsh noticed and reached out to pat her hand. "Don't worry, Annie. Hal's never down long—physically or mentally. He just doesn't have anything to do right now but lay around and think."

"Hospital beds are pretty depressing," Annie agreed.

"Are you speaking from your experience as a nurse?" Marsh turned right off the two-lane and headed his vehicle in the direction of the camp, now only minutes away.

"No," Annie replied. "As a patient."

"Yeah? When?"

"When I was eight. A train hit the car in which I was riding. Killed my parents and my little brother. Somehow, I survived with no more than a broken arm."

"God, Annie. I'm sorry. I never knew." Annie heard his distress.

She shrugged it away. "It was a long time ago. So long that I don't remember anything about it except lying in my hospital bed and worrying that I was going to lose Marie Michelle, too."

He stopped the Jeep in the drive of Timbertop and killed the engine, then turned slightly in the seat to look her in the eye. "Marie Michelle?"

"My doll."

"Oh." Marsh sat in silence for a second, then shook his head in obvious sympathy. "Poor Annie."

"Don't waste your pity on me," she told him. "Most kids have only two parents. I've had so many that I've lost count."

Marsh's silence lasted longer this time and ended with a soft sigh that could have meant anything. "It's not the quantity that matters."

"What do you mean?" Annie asked, though she thought she knew.

"I had one parent, myself, and as long as she lived, she did a great job raising me."

So he'd never had a dad. That explained his bonding with Hal. "What happened to your mother?"

"She was killed by a drunk driver."

"What a waste," Annie murmured, blinking back the tears of sympathy that sprang instantly to her eyes. "How old were you?"

"Six."

"That's the year you came to Timbertop for the first time, wasn't it?"

Marsh nodded. "Mom was killed on New Year's Eve. My grandparents sent me here in May."

He had grandparents? Annie had assumed he was on his own just as she was. "I didn't realize you had family," she murmured.

"A grandmother, a grandfather, two aunts and uncles, plus assorted cousins..."

Annie caught her breath, thoroughly surprised and downright envious. "Lucky you."

"Yeah...lucky me." Marsh's voice was flat. Swiveling in the seat, he opened the vehicle door and stepped out. "Coming?"

"Oh, um, yes." Annie scrambled out, too, and together they walked to the house. Nothing was said until they reached the door—probably because Annie was busy trying to assimilate Marsh's news.

Her head spun with questions. She wondered about his grandparents. Were they still living? And if so, where? And what about the rest of his family...those aunts, uncles and cousins? Marsh had such an independent air about him, Annie had always assumed he was an orphan, too. Then there was the little matter of his missing dad....

"Marsh?" They'd reached the kitchen door and she fumbled through her leather purse for the key.

"Hmm?"

"I was just wondering..." Annie's fingers closed around the elusive ring of keys. She pulled them free of the purse and stuck the appropriate one in the lock. "What I mean is..." She twisted the key, pushed open the door, then smoothly stepped in front of it and turned to face Marsh, blocking his way inside the house. "If you had so many relatives to care for you, why did you spend the entire summer at Timbertop?

Hal once told me you came every May and stayed through August.''

The instant Annie blurted the question, a possible reason sprang to mind: poverty. Hal did take a lot of charity campers, Annie Winslow included. And while her past financial status didn't bother her one bit, Marsh's certainly might bother him . . . and undoubtedly did, if his thunderous frown were any indication.

"I—I'm sorry," Annie stammered. "I guess that's really none of my business, is it?"

"No," Marsh replied rather coolly.

Contrite now, Annie stepped out of his way so he could go inside. But instead of doing that, Marsh turned on his heel and walked to the edge of the deck, where he sat lightly on the wooden rail that surrounded it. He looked out over Timbertop, then at Annie, before patting the rail beside him and motioning for her to walk on over to him.

She did, but somewhat slowly and feeling rather awful for raising such a delicate issue. "I can tell you think I was one of Hal's charity campers," Marsh said, his gaze back on their verdant surroundings.

Annie quickly nodded. "There's nothing wrong with that. I was one, myself, you know."

"Yeah, well there's poverty and then there's poverty." He shifted his solemn gaze from the terrain to Annie. "I didn't come to Timbertop because my grandparents couldn't afford to feed me at home," Marsh told her. "But I was a charity case, all the same, desperately in need of—"

"Love?"

"Actually, I was going to say emotional support."

That didn't surprise Annie, who doubted that Marsh would ever admit he needed love just like everyone else in the world.

"As for my family—" the word had a bitter ring to it "—they never cared for me other than financially. The only reason they took me in was to keep up appearances with their friends."

"So your grandparents are wealthy?"

"Ever heard of Clayton Cramer Cassidy the Third?"

"The photographer of the stars? Who hasn't?"

"Meet Gramps." The word dripped with sarcasm.

"Wow!" Well aware that the said Mr. Cassidy was one of the ten wealthiest businessmen in the nation, Annie swallowed hard and gave Marsh a shaky smile. "Must be where you got your photography talent, huh?"

"Well, I don't think I inherited it from dear old Dad."

"You knew him?"

"We never met, if that's what you're asking. I know he was a sailor and that he and my mother married on impulse while he was on a Cinderella liberty. I also know that once he returned to his ship, he never came back or answered my mother's letters. My grandparents tried to talk her into an abortion when they found out she was pregnant, but Mom was eighteen and old enough to decide for herself. Luckily for me, she had spunk and respect for life."

"Your mother told you all of this?" It was hard to believe a six-year-old would be privy to such details.

"Actually, I learned the cold, hard facts from my dear, sweet grandma, who shoved them down my throat at least twice a day."

He laughed when he told Annie that, but she wasn't fooled. His eyes glittered with his pain, and so without thought, she rose, stepped over one of his outstretched legs and threw her arms around his neck.

Marsh tensed. "What are you doing?"

"Hugging the hurt away," she replied, her words muffled by his shirtfront.

Marsh gave her no encouragement, but didn't pull back. And after what felt like an eternity, he actually wrapped his arms around Annie's waist in an embrace so tight the air whooshed from her lungs and her body molded to his.

Another eternity passed before Annie loosened her hold on him just enough to lean back so she could look him in the eye. "Miss Opal did this much better than I do."

"Oh, I don't know about that," Marsh replied. "You're doing a damn good job, yourself."

Annie laughed softly at his words, and Marsh laughed with her—a warm, honest sound that was music to her ears. Still holding Annie tightly against his body, Marsh stood, kissed her soundly on the mouth, then slowly lowered her until her feet touched the boards again.

And though her feet dutifully crossed those solid wooden planks to enter the house moments later, Annie's head stayed in the clouds for hours...right up until she pulled opened Opal's desk drawer to look for the checkbook Hal had mentioned that morning.

"Marsh! Get in here!"

Clearly hearing the distress in her cry, Marsh burst into the parlor in seconds.

"What's wrong?"

"Look."

He did, but didn't realize what he saw. "Bank statements?"

"Over a year's worth. They haven't even been opened except for last month's, and I opened it myself."

Marsh considered that before shrugging it away. "Hal did say he wasn't a bookkeeper."

"Then he needs to hire one," Annie said. "Get a load of this ending balance."

Marsh did, and his jaw dropped. "Sixty-two dollars and twelve cents?"

"Exactly."

"It can't be right. He must have another account somewhere."

"There's not another checkbook," Annie replied. "I've already looked."

Marsh took the bank statement from Annie's trembling hand and walked over to plop down on the couch. Clearly still confused, he stared at the paper for a full minute without speaking. "I don't get it."

"Neither do I. Why would Hal tell me he'd write checks for the pump and dishwasher if he knows he doesn't have funds to cover them?"

Marsh stood, walked over to the desk where Annie still sat, and riffled through the stack of statements now strewn across it. "None of these have been opened."

"I told you that a minute ago."

"Yeah, but it's just now registering with me," Marsh said, "along with a possible reason why Hal isn't worried about his money."

Annie's eyes rounded. "You mean..."

Marsh nodded. "He doesn't know he's broke." Marsh scanned the piece of paper he held. "It looks as though his social security check is his only source of income, and it's deposited directly into his account. I see that most of his bills are paid electronically, too, and that the bank has transferred some money from a savings account—twice last month—probably to cover these automatic withdrawals."

"Does the statement indicate the balance of his savings account?" She stood and pressed close to peruse the document. "There it is...oh, no." Annie stepped away and sank back into the chair just as Marsh's gaze found the shockingly low balance.

"Damn!"

They exchanged a glance; then Marsh tossed down the bank statement and walked over to the window. He looked through it, but dark as it was outside he could only see his own reflection in the glass. Nonetheless he didn't move for several silent moments.

"Should I call Hal?" Annie asked.

"I don't think so. I'm not sure he's up to handling problems this big."

"Not so big," Annie replied. "I mean...I can pay for the dishwasher if you can pay for the pump."

"Annie, honey, the dishwasher and pump are the least of our worries," Marsh growled. "I'm talking about the cook and the counselors who are arriving tomorrow. Who's going to pay them?''

"We'll get camping fees come Sunday...." She barely got the words out, so dry was her mouth and throat. "They should cover food, electricity and salaries with dollars to spare."

Marsh's expression instantly brightened. "That is a thought. I'd forgotten he doesn't make the campers pay when they register." In two strides he stood at the desk, opening and shutting drawers in an obvious search for something.

"What are you looking for?"

"The camp files. Opal used to keep them around here some place."

"Not in this desk," Annie told him. She pointed to a wooden file cabinet nearby. "In there. Top drawer."

In seconds Marsh was seated on the couch again, and this time he studied the contents of a file folder.

"Com'ere," he said to Annie after a short silence.

Her heart in her throat—Marsh looked more worried, if anything—Annie did as requested. What she saw was a list of the campers who would arrive on Sunday. Beside each name was a notation of what they owed.

"Is that what he charges for the whole week?" he asked, pointing to a ridiculously small figure.

"I—I don't know," Annie stammered. "I never had to pay..."

"Well, I paid—or my grandmother did—and that is exactly what Hal charged us twenty years ago!"

"Are you telling me he hasn't raised his price in all those years?"

"Looks that way," Marsh replied. "And it looks as though you aren't the only one who never had to pay. Take a gander at this...." He tapped the page with his forefinger, pointing out that more than half of next week's campers would owe nothing.

Clearly Hal still took in strays. And while this was a noble, needed gesture—one from which Annie, herself, had benefited—it would not pay the bills.

"What are we going to do?" she finally asked, her heart heavy with worry.

"I don't know, but we'd better think of something—" Marsh heaved a sigh "—and quick."

Since Annie could only agree, they put their heads together and talked deep into the night, trying to find a way to save the camp they both loved.

Marsh's suggestions were simple and short-range: raise the camping fee, increase the number of children each session, cut back on staffing.

Annie's, on the other hand, were much more complicated and farsighted: keep the camp going all year by opening its gates to church groups, senior citizens and the handicapped.

Marsh listened to her ideas without comment, a half smile on his face. Only when she finally stopped to breathe did he say anything and that was only because she demanded outright to hear his opinion.

"I think you have vision, Annie Winslow," he said. "But..."

"But what we need right now is money. And while the changes you suggest would almost certainly result in increased revenue in a few years, the truth is, we don't have that kind of time." Still seated on the couch where he'd sat for the past several hours, Marsh took a sip of his coffee, then shifted his attention back to Annie. "Do you understand what I'm saying?"

"I'm no dimwit," she informed him from her usual resting place, Opal's velvet chair. Annie sat sideways in that old chair, her back and knees supported by the armrests. "I realize that expanding the focus of Timbertop will cost before it pays...unless there's a second mortgage—"

Marsh snorted his opinion of that idea. "Be realistic. What bank is going to loan money to a man Hal's age?"

"Lot's of banks...if he has a younger cosigner."

"Younger cosigner, huh? And do you know any saint willing to take on that kind of commitment and risk?"

"She's not a saint by any means—just a woman who wants to help Hal as much as he helped her."

He looked surprised. "You?"

"Me." She gave him a hesitant smile.

Marsh tensed. "But, Annie—"

"But nothing. I'm gainfully employed and have some money in the bank. I should be a good credit risk."

"Your gainful employment is at Timbertop, the very camp that's in trouble. That might be a big minus on your loan application."

"Not if there's another cosigner—one whose livelihood doesn't depend on Timbertop."

"I guess you have someone in mind."

Annie nodded.

"A he?"

She nodded again.

Marsh grew very still and his eyes narrowed with suspicion. "Do I know this he?"

"Intimately," she told him, a word that chilled him as thoroughly as a drenching in ice water.

Chapter Five

"Forget it," Marsh said the moment he recovered from the shock. "I can't take on that kind of responsibility. I have too many obligations already—financial and otherwise."

"Oh, well. It was worth a try."

"It's not that I don't want to help Hal. I do, but not by cosigning a mortgage."

"It's okay, Marsh. It was just an idea. A stupid idea."

Stupid? Not really. Impossible? Absolutely...at least for Marsh McGriffey. Used to being on the move, he could barely imagine hanging around Timbertop until Hal's return, much less long enough to ensure the success of such an extended investment as a mortgage.

"You've got the right idea, but the wrong man. I'm...sorry."

"Don't be. I'm sure we can find another way to raise some quick cash." She stood, stretched lazily and moved toward Opal's ornate cuckoo clock, mounted on the papered wall. Expertly, she wound it, then she turned back to Marsh. "Maybe I could sell my body."

Annie's comment, no doubt uttered to lighten the moment, was not a bit funny to Marsh. "You'd better be joking," he growled, words that clearly surprised his companion.

"Of course, I'm joking," she replied with an incredulous laugh. "We're not that desperate yet, and who'd pay good money for a skinny redhead with freckles, anyway?"

"No man in his right mind," Marsh replied.

"Excuse me?" Teasing or not, she obviously considered his reply an insult.

He hurried to clarify it. "Only a fool would think he could afford so precious a gift."

Dead silence greeted those candid words. Then Annie gave him a sweet smile.

"That is surely the nicest thing any man ever said to me," she murmured, walking back to stand in front of him. "Thanks, Marsh." Bending down, she brushed a kiss lightly over his lips—a kiss he felt clear to his toenails. "I'm going to bed now. Will you lock all the doors?"

"No problem." Unless these wobbly knees are a permanent affliction.

"Good night, then. Sweet dreams."

"You have some, too."

"Oh, I plan on it," she assured him before vanishing into the hall.

As tightly wound as that old cuckoo clock, Marsh wasn't so sure he'd be similarly blessed. In fact, sleep was the last thing on his mind at the moment. He felt restless, sexually frustrated and, darn Annie's hide, guilty.

Not that he really believed there was a bank around that would loan the three of them money. In truth and in spite of Annie's optimism, Marsh sincerely doubted that.

No, his guilt stemmed from the knowledge that he could probably get the money from another source: his grandfather. Alienated from his grandson or not, Clayton Cassidy would almost certainly invest in Timbertop. He was no fool, after all, and Hal's land boasted some beautiful mountain acreage.

Unfortunately, Marsh's stomach churned at the mere thought of facing his grandfather again. Old memories of their last encounter, some fifteen years ago at Marsh's high-school graduation, filled his head. As though it were yesterday, he remembered his grandfather's shock when he learned that Marsh was responsible for the collage of candid senior photographs that served as backdrop to the ceremonies.

Clayton had actually complimented his grandson—a fond memory—then made him an offer of cold, hard cash to set up a portrait studio of his own. Marsh had flatly refused the offer, of course, and taken great pleasure in doing it—an even fonder memory.

Though only a teenager, Marsh had recognized this ploy to keep him out of the family business. And he'd been smart enough to feel insulted that the old man didn't consider him real competition.

Never mind his adult suspicions that youthful pride had blinded him....

Not for anyone—even Hal—would Marsh beg for money. Why, the very idea made his blood run cold. For that reason, he vowed to keep this last-resort tactic to himself. Annie, with her marvelous capacity for love and forgiveness, would never understand the bitterness that ruled his relationship with his grandparents.

She would expect him to rebuild bridges long since burned, then trot back over them as though nothing had happened. And softie that he was—at least where Annie was concerned—Marsh would find himself trying to please her even though he was no emotional engineer.

Upstairs in the dark of her bedroom, Annie also analyzed their last encounter.

First, she lamented not having the guts to suggest that Marsh turn to his family for the money. Common sense suggested the plan; women's intuition told her Marsh thought of it, too. But he hadn't volunteered for the mission, and, for some reason, she couldn't ask him to—a sure indication her loyalties were a bit mixed.

Second, she regretted her rash comment about selling her body. Who'd have thought Marsh would take it so seriously? Now he probably thought she didn't have any self-confidence when, in reality, she had plenty.

Not necessarily about her physical desirability, true, but certainly about other things. Specifically... Um...

Annie frowned into the dark for several minutes, desperately trying to think of an area of her life in which she possessed utter confidence. She heaved a sigh of relief when she finally thought of it: goals. Annie Winslow considered herself very goal-oriented and had every confidence she would achieve all she set out to do.

And why shouldn't she? She'd accomplished her biggest goal already obtaining a nursing degree. That was no small achievement for a penniless orphan.

As for the others—marriage, children—they, too, would be realized in time.

Not if you hide out in Timbertop, a still, small voice piped up from the back of Annie's mind.

"I'm not hiding," she said aloud, used to that nagging intonation some referred to as a conscience. Annie preferred to believe the voice was that of her mother, looking down from heaven, trying to guide her orphaned child. And like most children, Annie sometimes ignored the advice of said parent.

You mean you honestly think your Mr. Right is going to find you way out here?

"It's not entirely inconceivable," Annie retorted. "We do have visitors. Why, today alone we had three delivery men, one of whom was a real looker."

And very married.

"So? We get eligible bachelors out here, too."

Yeah? Name one.

"I'll be glad to. There was...uh..." Annie sat up in bed, as though that would help her think, and clasped her hands around her knees. "Hmm..."

I told you so.

"Just give me a minute, will you?" She squeezed her eyes tightly shut, desperate to come up with a name to justify her lack of social life. Instantly a vision of her former counselor and current housemate sprang into her head. "Marsh McGriffey. He's eligible."

But not the marrying kind.

"I'm not so sure of that."

Annie, Annie. What are you doing? The voice was fading.

"Nothing for you to worry about."

Be smart with your heart. This was a mere whisper.

"Always."

"Annie?"

"What?" she snapped before she realized that the voice calling out to her now belonged not to the spirit world or her conscience, but a flesh-and-blood man who'd probably heard her babbling to herself. How embarrassing.

"Sorry to disturb you. I thought I heard voices."

"Maybe it was my television," Annie suggested, crossing her fingers to negate the lie.

"You can't sleep?" Marsh sounded closer now, and Annie guessed he stood in the connecting bathroom. Would a little encouragement find him in her bedroom? she wondered.

And if it did, what would happen next?

Be smart with your heart.

Annie took a deep breath. "I couldn't sleep when I first came up, but I think I can now."

"Oh."

"Good night, Marsh."

She heard his sigh. "'Night, Annie."

* * *

Surprisingly enough, Annie slept deeply that night and woke refreshed on Saturday morning. Bright, golden sunlight bathed her bed. Reluctant to rise, she kicked back the crisp cotton sheets, closed her eyes again and basked in the glow without moving another muscle.

"Yo! Sleeping Beauty!" It was Marsh, of course, and sounding awfully close.

But Annie couldn't open her sleepy eyes. "Hmm?"

"Wake up. You've got a call."

With effort, Annie did as requested and found Marsh standing beside her bed, the cordless telephone in his hand. Instantly she was wide awake and scrambling to pull the sheet up over her satin gown.

She sat up, sheet clutched to her chest, and reached for the phone, grimacing at Marsh when he grinned at her. "Hello?"

"Is this Annie Winslow?"

"It is."

"Good. My name is Paula Harrison. My brother and I are counselors at Timbertop."

"I remember. Hal told me you two would be arriving this afternoon. I can't wait to meet you."

"Yes, well, that's what I'm calling about, I'm afraid. We've had a death in our family—" She made a choking sound "—my father. We won't be able to get there until sometime next week. I'm not sure when."

"That's perfectly all right," Annie quickly assured her even as her own eyes filled with tears. "I understand, and I want you two to take as long as you need. We'll be all right until you get here."

"You're positive?"

"Yes. Don't worry about a thing."

"Thanks a lot," Paula said.

"You're welcome," Annie replied, adding, "Paula?"

"Yes, ma'am?"

"I'm really very sorry about your dad. I know you'll miss him."

"Yeah."

Blinking to clear her vision, Annie turned off the telephone moments later and turned her attention to Marsh, who had not moved from where he stood by the bed. "You know what's happened?"

"I can guess."

"She sounded really upset," Annie said, swallowing hard.

Marsh nodded again.

"Maybe I'll just bake a cake to take over to their house. I know they live in town."

"Ah, Annie." The words sounded like a sigh of deep longing.

"What is it, Marsh?"

"You're just like a sponge—absorbing everyone else's pain." To Annie's astonishment, he then dropped down on the side of the bed and tugged her into his warm embrace.

"What are you doing?" Annie asked as she rested her cheek on his thudding heart.

"Hugging the hurt away, a skill I just learned from you."

"I don't think I ever did it this well," she murmured, relishing the feel of his hands rubbing lazy circles on her back.

He chuckled. "I always was a quick study."

Annie said nothing else—just enjoyed the comfort. It felt good to be held by such strong arms. She loved the warmth of his breath on the top of her head, the masculine scent of his after-shave.

She told herself no harm could come of this closeness. It was all very innocent, after all. He was relaxed; she was relaxed.

Relaxed? Ha! As they had the night before, every nerve ending in her body responded to Marsh's proximity, and were soon thoroughly stimulated and alive with need. Annie found herself craving more than just his hug.

Oh so timidly, she raised her chin enough to press her lips to the pulse racing in his neck.

He caught his breath.

Annie liked that response. It made her feel... special. Desired. Shifting her position slightly, she loosened his embrace just long enough to tuck her heels underneath her. This raised her face level with Marsh's and, looking deep into his eyes, she touched her lips to his.

He shivered violently—another unexpected reaction—then surprised her even more by falling back onto the bed. Still locked in his arms, Annie naturally went with him and found herself where she'd never been before: lying fully on top of a man.

Instantly, her heart rate doubled.

But she didn't move... not an inch. Instead, she pressed closer and experienced what she'd only imagined until then—being the object of a man's sexual desire.

That he wanted her, she had no doubt. He wore only sweats, and his body was tense with his need.

His rasping breaths and the sweat beading his forehead were further proof, if she needed it, as were the kisses he planted all over her face and neck. He traced the mounds of her hips with his hands, and at once Annie realized the seriousness of her position...the possible—no, probable—ending to this little idle.

Be smart with you heart.

"Not to mention the rest of me," she murmured aloud.

"What?" The question was husky soft and bordered by kisses so potent that goose bumps danced down her arms.

"I—I have to get up now."

"What?" He tensed, but did not release her.

"I've started something I can't finish. I must get up."

Marsh let her go at once, and Annie rolled off him. Scrambling off the bed, she crossed over to the window, where she stood sucking in deep breaths to calm herself. Through lowered lashes, she risked a peek at Marsh, who groaned softly, sat up very gingerly, and did a little deep breathing of his own.

Several seconds passed, during which neither spoke. Then Marsh got to his feet and walked to the door.

"Are you angry with me?" Annie demanded of him when he would have vanished through it without saying a word.

He halted and turned to look her dead in the eye. "It wasn't your fault, Annie."

"But it was. I kissed your neck."

"While I was hugging you."

"But I kissed you last night, too."

"And I kissed you yesterday." He sighed. "Give it a rest, okay? If anyone is to blame, it's Hal. He's the reason we're sharing a roof in the first place."

"It is not Hal's fault. Why, he couldn't possibly have known we'd be so...so..."

"Hot for each other?"

Annie winced, but didn't bother to correct him. "I mean, I didn't even know until..."

"I jumped your bones?"

"This isn't your fault."

"And it isn't yours, either, okay?" He leaned tiredly against the doorjamb and looked at her for a long time before he spoke again. "What say we start over?"

"You mean pretend this never happened?" She couldn't believe her ears.

Marsh nodded. "In a matter of hours, Ms. Potter and the other counselors will arrive. The kids will get here tomorrow. We won't have another minute to ourselves."

"Which is a darn good thing," Annie muttered, now thoroughly disgusted with her behavior the past half hour.

Marsh grinned at that. "So what do you say, Red? Are we friends and nothing more?"

Friends and nothing more. How sad, Annie thought as something very like regret pierced her heart. Nonetheless she nodded. "Friends and nothing more."

"Good. Now what are we going to do about our delayed counselors?"

"Delayed? Oh, yeah." When Marsh hugged hurt away, he really hugged it away. "I think that the state requires a one-to-six counselor-camper ratio."

"And we have how many more counselors coming today?"

Annie held up two fingers.

"Then it's hire two temporaries or do it ourselves, right?"

"Looks that way."

"Know of any possibles?"

"No, but Hal might."

Marsh shook his head. "Let's leave him out of this, okay?"

Annie saw the wisdom of that. "Okay."

"And let's forget hiring stand-ins. After all, we aren't even sure we can pay the regulars."

"Too true."

"I'll take the boys. You take the girls."

"How original."

Marsh laughed and so did Annie. When the sounds of their amusement died away, their gazes locked and his smile faded away.

"Is something wrong?" Annie asked, keenly attuned to his mood swing.

"Yes. I mean, no..." He laughed again, this time without humor. "Nothing's wrong, Annie. I was just wishing you weren't so damn beautiful."

Hours later, Annie still glowed from the warmth of that casual compliment and their aborted lovemaking. Who'd have believed Marsh was capable of such tenderness, such...heat?

Not Annie, and try as she might, she could not get it out of her head or heart so she could concentrate on what had to be done at Timbertop that day.

Then Ms. Potter arrived.

On crutches.

Annie, halfway down the deck steps and all ready to hug her old friend, stopped short at the sight. "Oh, my God. What happened?"

Bertha Potter, struggling with the aluminum crutches tucked under her arms, merely rolled her eyes in obvious disgust.

"She sprained it," explained Trevor Potter, the son who'd driven her up to Timbertop. A local grocery distributor, he supplied their food needs, so he walked around to the back of his station wagon and began to unload the boxes.

Marsh, just approaching them from behind the chow hall, began to assist, stopping only when waylaid by Ms. Potter.

"I can't believe it!" she exclaimed. "Marsh Mc-Griffey, and looking just like he did the last time I laid eyes on him."

Annie laughed at Marsh's pained expression. "And when was that?"

"Three—no, four years ago, I think. He stopped by to see Missus Opal and Hal during the last week of camp." Bertha kissed Marsh's flushed cheek, then leaned back slightly to give him a once-over. "Yes, just like he did back then. So big and tall." She focused on his face. "As handsome as alw— Hmm. On closer look, there's something different about you. Something I can't quite put my finger on...." Suddenly Bertha gasped. "You're in love, aren't you?"

"M-me?" he stammered, visibly taken aback.

"Yes, you," Bertha retorted. She smiled conspiratorially at Annie. "Hal used to worry about this boy, but I knew he'd fall sooner or later." She included Marsh in her smile. "Any man as good with kids as you, had to have a heart of pure mush."

"Oh, please," a red-faced Marsh muttered, a reply that sent Bertha into peals of laughter.

"Am I embarrassing you?" she asked, clearly pleased by the idea.

"Of course you are," growled her son Trevor as he brushed past with a box of groceries. His manner seemed to indicate he'd been on the receiving end of Bertha's good humor a time or two himself.

"Good," the cook then said to Marsh, adding, "Embarrassment is a healthy, human emotion that proves what I always knew. There's hope for this lone wolf, here." She patted Marsh on the shoulder. "Who is your woman, by the way? Anyone I know?"

Marsh, recovering somewhat, just shook his head as though to indicate he had no intention of telling anything. He then made a quick escape indoors, leaving Annie to wonder if there really was a mystery woman back in Atlanta, Marsh's usual stomping grounds.

That would certainly explain his "friends and nothing more" suggestion.

At three o'clock the other two counselors hired by Hal arrived. Both seasoned and hard workers, Ginger Welty and Shane Phillips knew exactly what to do and jumped right in to help Annie, Marsh and Ms. Potter with last-minute chores and details.

The sun set before Annie and Marsh left camp for the hospital, and by the time they climbed out of the

Jeep and headed up to Hal's room, it was completely dark.

Both were a little nervous. They planned to discuss finances, after all, as well as future plans for Timbertop—sensitive subjects at any time, downright touchy subjects tonight.

But when Hal greeted them with a glum smile and the news that his surgery had been postponed until Tuesday, Marsh and Annie tabled their discussion by mutual, unspoken consent. Instead, they reminisced about the summer Annie and Marsh met.

Eyes sparkling, Annie reminded Hal of the turtle she'd found in the creek that meandered through the campgrounds. Round as a quarter, green as a blade of grass, that precious pet had accompanied Annie to her first three foster homes.

"I remember your turtle," Hal commented, laughing. "Didn't you name him Popeye?"

Clearly pleased to see Hal in better spirits, Annie smiled and nodded. "I can't believe you remembered that."

Hal smiled back. "A turtle named Popeye is rather unforgettable, honey." He looked at Marsh. "You fished a lot that summer, didn't you?"

"Yeah," Marsh replied. "And usually with a red-headed pest who always knew the minute I headed for the storage shed to get a pole."

"I like that!" Annie exclaimed, adding a playful punch to Marsh's chin.

He ducked and captured her wrists in his hands, a move that held her immobile and only inches away. Instantly he was hot for her, and only the knowledge that Hal watched their "fight" with avid interest and much amusement kept Marsh from stealing a kiss.

Annie didn't seem to notice his tension. She just twisted free and laughed with Hal over some silly something—Marsh didn't know what.

The visit seemed to drag on forever, probably because he needed time alone. All afternoon—ever since Ms. Potter's erroneous and embarrassing assumptions regarding the state of his heart—he'd wished for solitude. But that was a precious commodity and would be for the next three months.

Three months? What was he thinking of? He'd be gone in three weeks—sooner if Hal did well.

Tuning out Hal's and Annie's chatter, Marsh closed his eyes and imagined his apartment in Georgia. Spacious, modern, it was the perfect bachelor pad—a place he'd picked with care and loved.

A man could find plenty of solitude in that apartment. Too much, now that he thought about it.

Too much? Could a man ever have too much time alone?

Only if he became used to company—Marsh's secret fear and the very reason Ms. Potter's talk of his falling in love had so alarmed him. What if Annie had taken Bertha's chatter seriously? What if she thought Marsh had fallen in love with her? It would be a natural assumption considering their early morning bedroom activities. And in light of the goals she had shared with him down by the lake Thursday night, she might now be hoping for commitment he was incapable of giving.

"Marsh, are you asleep?"

With a start, Marsh opened his eyes and sat bolt upright in the chair. "Not asleep. Just daydreaming."

"It's night, son," Hal told him. "And from what Annie's been telling me, you've done the work of ten men. Why don't you two get on back to Timbertop, get yourselves some rest."

"Don't mind if I do," Marsh said, rising.

"And don't worry about coming to the hospital again until Tuesday, you hear? I'd rather have you two at camp, keeping those kids in line, than baby-sitting me."

Marsh and Annie agreed, and in minutes said their goodbyes and exited the hospital. Silently they walked to his Jeep. And just as silently they made the journey back to camp.

Or almost back.

Two miles from Timbertop and Ms. Potter's watchful eyes, Marsh suddenly detoured to a mountain lookout he knew well.

"Going to do a little stargazing?" Annie asked. Apparently she knew the area quite well, too.

"Actually, I'm going to postpone our return to camp."

"You don't want to go back?"

"Not just yet," Marsh replied, adding, "Do you mind?"

"No."

Three minutes later, Marsh braked the Jeep to a halt near a wall formed of natural rock. He and Annie climbed from the vehicle and walked together to look out over the midnight blue valley. The twinkling lights of scattered houses below matched the twinkling of the stars above. A mountain breeze ruffled Annie's hair and cooled Marsh's face. He let the peace of their surroundings absorb him, and for the first time since early that morning, he relaxed.

Annie did the same, as evidenced by her deep sigh. "Isn't the silence awesome?"

"Yeah," he agreed, almost reluctant to break it with conversation. "Better make the best of it, I have a feeling this is the last time we'll be this alone, this relaxed for a long, long time."

Annie laughed softly at that. "I know."

Though Marsh could barely make out her expression in the dark, he sensed her regret, and it was almost his undoing. "You know something, Red? I think I'm going to miss you—quite an admission from a lone wolf like me."

"Ms. Potter didn't really mean that," Annie said, moving close enough to slip her arm through his in a gesture of comfort. She rested her chin on his biceps.

"I think she did," Marsh replied. "And I think she's right...at least about that. She's way off the mark in thinking I'm in love, though."

"You don't have some gorgeous blonde waiting in your bed back home?"

So Annie had not assumed she was his love. What a relief.

Or was it? Marsh instantly wondered.

Chapter Six

"No blonde in my bed," Marsh muttered, for some reason a bit disgruntled. Did Annie think he took sex that casually?

"She's a brunette?"

"I don't have a lover, Annie. I keep to myself."

"Oh." She released him and walked over to the rock wall, on which she sat, her back to the panoramic view. "I do, too... at least romantically."

Now what was that supposed to mean? Marsh wondered, and was suddenly consumed with a desire to find out. "You haven't, um, dated a lot? A beautiful woman like you?"

"Dated as in slept around?" she asked, not fooled by his wording.

"Mmm-hmm."

"That's a rather personal question, don't you think?"

"Yeah," Marsh agreed, adding, "And you don't have to answer it if you don't want to."

"Oh, I don't mind admitting I'm inexperienced," Annie told him. "I don't think traditional values are anything to be ashamed of."

"Neither do I," Marsh said, and he meant it. He smiled to himself, pleased to know exactly why Annie had pushed him away that morning. All day he'd wondered about it.

"Does that mean you haven't experimented, either?"

Marsh winced. "I'm afraid I can't go that far."

"I . . . see." She sounded disappointed, and immediately Marsh found himself on the defensive.

"I'm not into casual sex, though."

"You've loved the women you slept with?"

"I didn't exactly love them. It was more like a . . . need." He swallowed hard. "Sometimes I get really lonely, Annie."

"And do you feel better after you sleep with a stranger?"

He searched his soul for the answer to that and didn't like what he found there. "No."

"Poor Marsh."

"What the hell is that supposed to mean?" Marsh demanded, walking over to stand in front of her, fingertips stuffed into the back pockets of his jeans. There was nothing he hated more than pity. And coming from Annie, it was intolerable.

She shrugged, a movement dipped in moonlight. "I mean that I'm sorry you never learned that sex cannot replace love."

"Maybe not," Marsh retorted, "but it can be a hell of a lot of fun."

"So that's all we were doing this morning, having a little fun?"

Marsh flinched, but didn't correct her. How could he without admitting to himself—and to Annie—how much she meant to him? "You thought we were doing something else?"

"I guess not," she admitted. "I just hoped . . ."

"Ah, Annie. What do you want from me?"

"I'm not sure," she told him with a forced laugh. "But if I ever figure it out, I'll let you know. Now could we please go back to camp. I'm cold." She hugged her arms and shivered.

Marsh, every bit as chilled if not from the breeze, willingly agreed.

He expected their relationship to be radically different and, in fact, worried about it the rest of the way home. But Annie—warm-hearted Annie—soon chased that fear away by bidding him a sweet good night just the same as always before she turned in.

That demonstrated a remarkable understanding of the problems he had opening up, Marsh decided.

Or did it mean she'd given up on him?

Suddenly depressed, Marsh headed to his own bed, from where he listened to the sounds of Annie's sleep—a soft sigh, a creaking bedspring, a sob.

A sob? Concerned, Marsh slipped from his bed and moved without sound through the bathroom to Annie's doorway. He peered in and, since his eyes were already adjusted to the dark, instantly made out the form of Annie, curled up and asleep, if her steady breaths were any indication.

If she cried, it was in her sleep, he realized. And wishing more pleasant dreams for her, he returned to his lonely bed.

At ten o'clock the next day, Sunday, Annie looked out the kitchen window and watched the first campers pull through Timbertop's gate.

By noon that same day, all twenty-four had arrived and were traipsing to the chow hall for their first meal. Overhead, gathering storm clouds threatened the rain long promised by the weatherman. But the children, all bubbling with excitement, never even noticed.

Since Marsh had put new tops on four of the tables and removed the others from the chow hall—one of the last-minute chores that had kept him occupied the day before—six children and a counselor were assigned to each.

Annie noticed that Marsh's camera hung from a colorful strap around his neck and then laughed when he realized she'd spotted it. Marsh just gave her a sheepish grin, raised the camera, and snapped her picture—an action that caught her off guard, but pleased her.

Annie's charges, six girls ranging in age from seven to ten, consumed their lunch of hot dogs, potato chips and fruit cocktail as though it were their last, then headed with glee to the hobby hut, next activity on a busy agenda.

Before following them into the hut, Annie watched Marsh lead his crew to the lake, where they would learn water safety and be tested for swimming skills.

He looked especially wonderful today, she decided. Probably because she could not have him. Wasn't the grass always greener when out of reach?

"Miss Annie! Miss Annie!"

Jerked from her maudlin musings, Annie joined her campers, already up to their necks in scissors, glue, watercolors, construction paper and who knew what else.

Quickly she issued orders and got them under control. And within an hour, every child had finished a decoration to be hung in their "home in the woods," the next activity of the day.

"Diane, Melissa, Glenda, Judy, Jonni and Patricia. Line up!" The names rolled off Annie's tongue, probably because they each wore an identification pin. "Now we're going to search for our hideaway. I want you to pair up and hold hands so no one gets lost."

Diane, ten-years-old and the senior of Annie's group, snorted at that. "Only babies get lost." She gave her raven ponytail a toss.

"That's why I want you to attach yourself to one, okay?" Annie replied, her voice lowered so the "babies" wouldn't be insulted.

As expected, Diane rose to the challenge and grabbed the hand of the youngest girl, Melissa, an orphan and one of Hal's charity campers. Blue-eyed and blond, she was as pretty as the doll she carried everywhere.

The other girls quickly followed suit and in minutes they tramped a familiar trail into the verdant woods that was Timbertop. Annie kept an anxious watch on the clouds overhead, but since rain didn't seem imminent she soon put that worry out of her head and eyed her rambunctious responsibilities with tolerance and some amusement.

Dressed in everything from jeans so blue and stiff they must have been new to shorts so worn they had to be hand-me-downs, the girls each wore a bright yellow, highly visible T-shirt emblazoned with the word Timbertop, which was set within an outline of the state of Virginia. Silhouetted trees at the beginning and end of the camp name completed the simple design.

Annie loved the shirts, created by a very artistic Opal years ago. And she wore her own with pride.

"Now remember," she called out to the children leading her. "We're looking for a home. We need a good, flat area for picnics, and we need someplace to sit. We also need some trees to hang our pictures on."

"If it rains, our pictures will get wet," said Patricia, an eight-year-old from Roanoke. Having read the biographies sent in with the campers' registration papers, Annie knew Pat's parents hailed from Mountainburg and wanted their only child to experience the same fun in the woods they once enjoyed.

"That's okay," Annie told her. "We can always make more."

Since that answer seemed to satisfy Pat and everyone else, they moved forward, each scanning the area for the perfect home.

"Look! Look!" Judy exclaimed not long afterward. She jumped up and down in her excitement, brunette braids flopping, and pointed off to the right at a perfect site for their "home."

Annie, who'd been heading for that particular spot all along, feigned interest and then pleasure before taking a vote to see if this was where the girls wanted to set up housekeeping. It was unanimous—a good thing, since Annie didn't intend to travel much farther into the woods.

From this particular "home" the girls could still see camp and, more important, camp could see them.

"Diane," Annie said. "Will you sweep, please?"

"You're going to sweep the ground?" The child looked incredulous, and Annie had to laugh.

"We are. Then we're going to gather up leaves and put them down as carpet." She reached up into a nearby tree and, with a little help from a pocketknife, severed a leafy branch from it, which she handed to Diane to serve as a broom.

She then helped the other girls nail their pictures to the "walls," an action that gave their one-room home a very cozy feel. Fallen logs were next located, dragged into the "room" and arranged to provide seating for the seven of them. Last came the dried-leaf strewing process, and by four o'clock that afternoon, construction of their hideaway was complete.

"So what do you think, girls?" Annie asked.

"It's bee-yu-tiful," Melissa replied, an answer that resulted in laughter all around. Annie let them sample the "chairs" just long enough to tell them a story, then herded everyone back to camp for cleanup before dinner.

Just as they entered the camp proper, so did Marsh and his boys. Annie gave him a quick once-over, anxious to see how he'd survived his day. It had been years since he'd done this sort of thing, after all.

He caught her glance and gave her a cocky grin and a wave before vanishing into the dorm he would share with all the other males—a sure sign he'd survived and even had a little fun in the bargain.

And though more experienced as a camper than a counselor, so had Annie. In fact, she now regretted that she had never worked for Hal in this capacity before. That would have been next to impossible, of course. She was too busy shuffling between foster homes.

"Miss Annie! There's bunches of spiders in here!"

Oh, boy, Annie thought, and hurried to join her girls inside their own quarters.

The "bunches of spiders" turned out to be two of the daddy longlegs variety. Though rather scary-looking, they were quite harmless, which Annie demonstrated by letting one crawl up her arm.

Soon all the girls—Ginger's included—had made friends with the arachnids. All but Jonni, that is. The honey blonde retreated to her bunk and watched their antics with wide eyes and an expression of utter disbelief.

By dinnertime, Annie could barely drag herself over to the chow hall. And it was with great relief that she plopped into her chair at the head of the table and rested her weary head in her hands.

Keep your elbows off the table, Annie W.!
Keep your elbows off the table, Annie W.!
We've seen you do it twice,
And it isn't very nice!
So keep your elbows off the table, Annie W.!

"Excuse me!" Annie exclaimed, quickly removing those guilty elbows. She risked a glance at Marsh, who winked and laughed, innocent movements Annie found quite appealing. He looked more relaxed than she'd ever seen him and remarkably at home, considering he was surrounded by his six squirming campers.

If men only knew how sexy they looked when they held a baby, played rough and tumble with a toddler, or hugged a grown son, she thought. Why, every one of them would borrow their nieces and nephews to take on dates.

And every one of those dates—softhearted women with a secret longing for the American dream—would soon find themselves hopelessly, sexually involved with a man who had no stronger motivation than need.

Be smart with your heart.

I am, I am, Annie silently replied. Today, anyway. I can't promise anything about tomorrow.

That admitted, she felt oddly better and turned her attention to Ms. Potter's vegetable soup. Hot, chock-full of potatoes, carrots, corn and chicken, it tasted every bit as wonderful as it smelled. And in seconds Annie thought of nothing else but eating.

Sometime after soup but before the chocolate cake, it began to rain. Annie didn't mind a bit, of course. She loved to hear rain in the treetops. And there was nothing so cozy as being high and dry during a storm.

Some of her girls didn't share her enthusiasm, unfortunately, and Annie soon found herself teaching them how to count between flashes of lightning and claps of thunder to ascertain how far away the electrical activity was. Though probably not scientifically accurate, that tactic had distracted countless children through the ages and did so tonight.

For that reason, it was six worry-free children who finally headed to their dorm, only to discover that the roof had leaked and water now puddled on their floor.

To make matters worse, the next flash of lightning resulted in a blackout—a sure indication of trouble somewhere along the rural power lines in the area.

The girls squealed, of course, but Annie and Ginger, a petite nineteen-year-old with a pearl-white smile and raven-black curls, soon calmed them. Annie located a flashlight—there were several in each dorm—and gave one to Diane, the oldest girl in both groups.

After instructing them all to stay put just inside the door, a dry area, Annie and Ginger loped next door for a conference with their male counterparts.

But things were no better on that side of camp, though the boys displayed a more stoic attitude about the whole thing. Water ran in rivulets down the walls. One of the bunks under a particularly large drip already sagged with the weight of the moisture.

Marsh took one look at Annie and Ginger, both soaked to the skin, and motioned for his boys to line up beside him.

"We'll meet you in the chow hall," he said, an executive decision with which no one argued. "Bring whatever bedding is dry."

While the men rounded up the boys and dry blankets, Annie and Ginger ran back to their dorm and did the same with the girls. Soon all twenty-four children stood in the chow hall, as did Ms. Potter who'd somehow managed her crutches and a flashlight long enough to limp through the rain to join them.

Marsh and Shane quickly put their boys to work dividing the room in two with the tables. All the counselors then supervised their charges in the arrangement of sheets, blankets and pillows.

Thoroughly distressed by this latest disaster, it took Annie almost half an hour to realize that everyone else was having a ball. Astonished, she sat back on her heels near her bedroll and watched her whispering, giggling girls, only belatedly realizing why they acted as silly as they did: the boys. Even Melissa, the "baby" of the group seemed extremely aware of who lay just beyond the tables now dividing the room.

Annie had to laugh, and when she did, the whole misadventure became fun for her, too.

"Annie?" It was Ms. Potter.

"Yes?"

"I think I remember seeing some kerosene lamps out in the storage building. Why don't you send a couple of those boys out to check."

"It's locked," Marsh said. With the room so noisy, Annie hadn't even heard his approach. "I'd better go." He extended a hand to Annie. "Come with me?"

"Um, sure," she murmured, accepting his help to stand. Together, they braved the lashing rain and made a dash to the storage room. And in seconds Annie ducked through the doorway.

Marsh followed on her heels, and to her astonishment kicked the weathered wooden door shut behind him. He then flicked off the flashlight.

"What are you doing?" Annie gasped as he reached out and drew her into his arms.

"Stealing a kiss," he told her. "And I didn't want Ms. Potter or anyone else to peek through the cracks in this old building to watch me do it."

"But yesterday you said you wanted us to be friends and nothing more," Annie reminded him.

"Annie, honey, I couldn't feel much friendlier than I do now," Marsh said, then took her in a hungry kiss.

She didn't resist. How could she when he felt, smelled and tasted so marvelously good?

"Ah, Annie," he breathed between kisses planted on her mouth, her eyes, her cheek. "You're driving me insane."

"Not on purpose," she gasped.

He laughed at that—laughed, tangled his fingers in her hair and kissed her again. "We need to go back. They're going to come looking for us if we don't."

Go back? He thought he could waltz her in here, kiss her senseless, and then go back. Damn the man and his "needs." Annie Winslow had a few of her own.

With a sound very much like a growl, she framed his face with her hands and tugged it down so she could kiss him. Brazenly, she traced his lips with her tongue, then probed his mouth for entrance.

Though obviously startled, he quickly rallied and allowed her access. And as she teased and tasted, he somehow managed to wrap his arms around her thighs, lifting her up until they were heart to heart, with his need pressed hotly, boldly, unmistakably to hers.

His hands were everywhere, touching, kneading, electrifying yet holding her tightly against him all the while. He stumbled back against the wall, an action

that threatened to bring the old building down around
their heads, but Annie barely noticed, so caught up in
the moment.

He groaned. She gasped. The wind rattled the tin
roof.

"I need you," he whispered.

That word again. Well, she needed him, too, and
quickly decided their mutual need shouldn't be de-
nied—even if it wasn't exactly what she'd always
dreamed of.

"Marsh? Are you in there?"

He tensed and touched his fingers to Annie's mouth
as though they could actually pretend they were not
there if neither replied.

Annie knew better and peeled his fingers from her
mouth. "Who is it?" she whispered.

"Phil," Marsh replied just as softly.

"The kid who's stuck to you like a leech all day?"
Ten years old, with hair as orange as a carrot, the child
in question clearly idolized his counselor.

"Yeah." Marsh released her then and stepped over
to the door. "Thank goodness you're here," he told
the child now standing just outside of it, flashlight in
hand. "The batteries are out in this darn light, and we
can't find a thing in here."

"I'll help." Eagerly, Phil stepped into the shed. He
spotted Annie at once and nodded, seemingly un-
aware that she deliberately avoided the direct beam of
his light. Flushed, frustrated, and already regretting
what she'd just done, Annie wasn't up to bright lights
and curious eyes at the moment.

"There they are," Marsh said, pointing to the kerosene lamps sitting square in the middle of the tiny

shed. If Phil thought they were idiots for not stumbling over the lamps, he said nothing. And he and Marsh soon made short work of gathering them up along with a can of kerosene with which to fuel them. "You lead the way out since you've got the light," Marsh instructed, motioning Phil to the door.

The child did as directed, stepping out into the rain and then dashing to the chow hall. Marsh and Annie followed, but not before he yanked her up in his arms and kissed her so hard it hurt.

"We'll continue this discussion in the very near future," he said, words that had a decidedly ominous ring to them. As useless as that transformer out on the highway, Annie couldn't think of a proper reply—one designed to neutralize this, their latest encounter—until she was surrounded by six hyperactive campers, one of whom directed the beam of her flashlight right on Annie's flushed face.

"What took you so long?" demanded Judy.

They'd been gone a long time?

"We thought you were lost," added Jonni.

As lost as a girl could get.

"Your hair's all tangled," Glenda chimed in.

So what else is new?

"And your lip's bleeding," added Melissa.

"It is?" Annie put her hand to her mouth, which still throbbed from Marsh's last kiss. "Oh, it is."

"I have a tissue," Diane said, handing her one that looked slightly used.

Annie took it and dabbed her lip. "Thanks, girls." She glanced around and found that Marsh and Shane had lighted the lamps, which gave off a soft, warm glow. "Please turn off the flashlight, Judy."

Judy did.

"Now I want you girls to get into your beds. It's very late, and we have a lot of fun things to do tomorrow."

"What if it rains again?" asked Melissa, who'd pulled her bedding so close that Annie was grateful she wasn't claustrophobic.

"We'll get wet, I guess," Annie told her, adding, "think you'll melt?"

"She ain't sweet enough," Diane answered, a reply that almost started a pillow fight.

But Annie took control of the situation, and because she did, her girls soon slumbered all around her.

Annie, of course, didn't fall asleep so quickly. She was too busy trying to analyze Marsh's latest actions.

What did he want from her? Surely not the friendship he claimed. Friends did not hide in the shed and steal kisses.

Did he then desire an affair? Annie wasn't sure but suspected that to be true. Since marriage was definitely not on his agenda, there could really be no other motive for his actions.

And how did she feel about that? Well . . . last week at this time, the mere thought would have scandalized Annie. Tonight she found herself wondering if an affair might not be the perfect solution to the dilemma of Marsh McGriffey.

She would have to compromise her goals, of course. She'd have to postpone her dreams of a fairy tale happily-ever-after. But maybe only temporarily if they had an affair and he fell in love.

Fell in love? Had she lost her mind? This was real life, not that fairy tale. Marsh wasn't going to fall in love with the likes of Annie Winslow.

He was a loner, a man skilled at hiding his emotions and guarding his heart. Their current circumstances—the proximity of their bedrooms, their mutual respect for Hal, their loyalty to Timbertop— might have lured him close enough to touch, but she would never, ever be able to hold him.

And that was okay, now that she thought about it. For Annie wasn't going to fall in love with him, either.

Monday dawned clear and bright, much to everyone's relief. After breakfast, Shane and Ginger directed all twenty-four campers in dormitory cleanup, then rewarded them with a noontime picnic by the lake.

While they ate, Annie helped Marsh repair the leaky roofs as best he could. Shane, of course, would probably have been a better assistant, but when she suggested it, Marsh nixed the idea. He wanted the boys to have male supervision, he claimed, an explanation Annie doubted the first time he backed her into the corner of the dorm and began to take up right where they'd left off the night before.

"What do you think you're doing?" Annie demanded, pushing him away.

"I think I'm kissing you," Marsh replied with a laugh.

"Well, you can just forget it. We have work to do." That said, Annie sashayed past and made it as far as the door before Marsh caught her by the belt loop and tugged her back into his arms.

"Is that the real reason you're resisting me?" he asked.

It wasn't, of course, and Annie suspected he could tell. "I'm afraid someone will see us."

"Who? The kids are at the lake. Ms. Potter is hanging sheets on the line. Look. You can see her."

"All right, then, I'll be honest. I don't want to kiss you."

"That's not the message I got last night," Marsh told her. "And that's not the message I'm getting now." He rubbed his thumb over the tip of her breast, traitorously taut and straining against her T-shirt.

Annie's cheeks flamed. "So maybe I do want to kiss you. I'm still not going to."

"Tell me why, Annie," he said. "I need to know."

"Need, smeed!" Annie exclaimed, twisting free of him. "I'm sick to death of hearing what you need. For your information, Marsh McGriffey, I have needs of my own, and a roll in the hay is not one of them."

Marsh glared at her. "Is that what you think I want?"

"It isn't?"

"No."

"Then what do you want?" Annie's heart pounded so loudly, she wondered if Marsh could hear it.

"I want...well..." Abruptly he sighed. "More than a roll in the hay, but less than what you probably want."

Annie digested that in silence, then laughed.

"What's so funny?" Marsh demanded, clearly affronted.

"You. Me." She laughed again, this time without humor. "What a mess."

Marsh could only agree with that. "I know I'm not good for you. And if it's any consolation, I've tried to keep my distance."

Annie smiled at the irony of that. "Thanks."

"Maybe I should leave. You'd probably be all right here. You do have help—"

"No!" She swallowed hard. "No."

"But this is torture for us."

"Then we'll just have to be strong. Hal needs you, Marsh, and he needs me, too. We can't let him down."

"I know." He said the right words, but didn't sound a bit convinced.

"We're in lust, not love," Annie reminded him. "No real damage has been done. We can still do the right thing."

"Which is?"

"Quit trying to reconcile our goals."

He thought about that a moment. "You're right, you know."

"Of course, I am. Will you stay?"

"I'll stay," he agreed. "But that's all I can promise."

"Are you warning me that I might find myself mouth to mouth with you again?"

Marsh gave her a wry grin. "Almost certainly. I'm a weak, weak man, Annie Winslow—especially where you're concerned."

"Oh, yeah? Well, don't worry too much about that. Contrary to appearances thus far, I'm really a strong, *strong* woman."

He winced. "Especially where I'm concerned?"

"Especially there, Marsh McGriffey," she lied. Especially there.

Chapter Seven

By the time Annie's girls headed to their dorms Monday night, all roof leaks had been repaired and the electricity was functional again.

She and Ginger ushered them into the showers, patiently reminded them to brush their teeth, then sent them to their prospective bunks for a half hour of unwinding before the lights were turned out.

It was during this time that counselors were to urge their charges to write home, and so Annie and Ginger did just that, cleverly loaning them pretty pastel writing paper as extra incentive.

At nine, the women reminded the girls to make a potty run, then tucked each of them into their beds. As Ginger settled in the last child, Jonni, Annie gave the area a quick inspection. She noted that all twelve girls were snug as bugs in a rug—six in top bunks, six in bottom bunks.

Finally Ginger gave Annie the all-finished signal. With a sigh of relief, Annie flicked off the light, only to turn it on again when one of the girls screeched bloody murder.

"What on earth..." Ginger exclaimed, dashing back toward the rear of the dorm, Annie on her heels.

"Wasps!" Jonni, the squeamish one, exclaimed, pointing.

Sure enough, there were wasps—swarming a massive nest on one of the exposed rafters crisscrossing the room. Since this particular rafter was right over Jonni's bed, she couldn't miss seeing the activity.

Immediately, all the girls squealed and leapt from their beds, surrounding Annie, friend of spiders, in a rush.

If she could cope with spiders so handily, then wasps would be a piece of cake, right?

Wrong.

Annie froze, her eyes widening in sheer horror. Nothing, but nothing, frightened her more than wasps. And there were so many!

With effort, she kept her voice calm. "It's all right, girls. Be cool." She turned to Ginger. "Keep them right here by the door. I'm going for help."

That said, Annie pulled a pair of shorts on under her sleep shirt, dashed out the door and headed straight for the boys' dorm. Halfway there, she heard more screams, and by the time she reached the male living quarters twelve campers and a counselor ran up behind her.

"They started chasing us!" Melissa breathlessly exclaimed, even as bright light illuminated the small concrete porch, and Marsh flung open the door.

"What in the he—er, heck is going on?"

Annie, struggling to keep from being pushed right into his arms by the girls crowding so close behind her, could barely reply. "Wasps."

"What?"

"Wasps. In our dorm."

"Oh." Was that a smile tugging at the corner of his lips? Though Marsh's amusement would have irritated Annie under normal circumstances, right now she just wanted him to rid her dorm of those flying, stinging varmints. "Want me to kill them?"

"Please."

"What is it? What is it?"

Now it was Marsh's turn to try to keep his balance. Behind him, clamoring to get outside, were twelve boisterous boys and a sleepy-eyed counselor.

"The other dorm has a little wasp problem."

"Girls are wimps," stated one of the boys with obvious disdain. Annie recalled that his name was Jerry. Stockily built, probably ten years old, there was no doubt the youngster held the opposite sex in low esteem.

"Yeah, wimps," echoed one of the other male campers. On closer inspection, Annie realized he had to be David, twin to the first.

"We are not!" yelled Diane, pushing her way to the front of the crush, clearly ready to do battle.

"Whoa now!" Marsh exclaimed, grabbing his rowdy boys by the scruff of the neck. In one smooth motion, he set them behind him. "I have a better idea than fighting. Let's build a bonfire, and while all of you are roasting marshmallows, I'll get rid of the wasps. Okay?"

"Yeesss!"

"Ginger, would you ask Ms. Potter for some marshmallows? I see that her light is still on." Bertha slept in the house proper, right off the kitchen, and with a nod, Ginger headed that way. Marsh turned his attention to Annie. "Think you can build a fire? Usual spot, of course."

"Sure." Quickly she rounded up her campers, then marched them to the woodpile, where she loaded each down with a log. She then directed the arrangement of those logs in the clear, sandy area always used for campfires.

While they worked, Marsh, Shane and their boys dealt with the wasps. The yells that emanated from the dorm were a source of great amusement to the girls. It seemed that females weren't the only ones who got a little nervous around insects that could fly and sting.

Annie's watch read nine-fifty before Marsh pronounced the dorm pest-free and gathered his boys around the brightly burning fire. Ms. Potter, who'd passed around marshmallows and roasting sticks, stayed to sample the delicacy, while Shane, a wanna-be writer, told a marvelous ghost story.

Thoroughly exhausted by now—supervising six girls and avoiding Marsh McGriffey was hard work!—Annie sat back from the fire so she could lean against a tall oak.

"Don't turn around."

The words were a whisper, coming from behind her tree, but Annie knew that Marsh uttered them.

"What is it?" she whispered back, scanning the preoccupied campers to see if anyone noticed her talking to the oak.

"I need, um, *want* to talk to you. Meet me in the parlor in five minutes."

Though of half a mind to ignore him, Annie could not resist the mysterious invitation. She waited four minutes, then oh so casually slipped away and walked to the house.

Marsh waited in the parlor, which was illuminated only by the light of the mercury vapor security lamp mounted on a utility pole outside.

"Don't," he said when Annie automatically reached to turn on the ceiling light. He gestured toward the open windows, through which the bonfire was plainly visible. "I want to keep an eye on the campers without them keeping an eye on us."

Baffled and by now a tad suspicious, Annie obeyed with reluctance. "What do you want?"

"To talk, just like I said." He patted the couch on which he sat, and when she hesitated to join him, added, "I swear."

Annie shrugged and sat...as close to the armrest as she could.

Marsh chuckled. "Are you scared of me?"

"No. I'm scared of *me*."

"I thought you were a strong woman, Red."

"Strong, but not invincible," she replied. "Now why did you ask me to meet you here? What is it you want to talk about?"

"Us."

Annie snorted. "There is no us."

"I know, and I'm not sure I like it."

Annie caught her breath. Her heart filled with hope. "What are you trying to say?"

"That I don't like the way you're avoiding me."

"So you noticed." That pleased her.

"Hell, yeah, I noticed."

"Well, what do you expect me to do?" Annie demanded. "We did agree to quit trying to reconcile our goals."

"I know we did."

"Do you know a better way to do it than staying out of each other's hair?"

"No."

"Then what's the problem?"

"I missed you today," Marsh retorted. "*That's* the problem."

He'd missed her... actually *missed* her. Annie's heart sang. "You have to care for someone to miss them, Marsh. Are you saying you care for me?"

"I guess I am."

"You know I care for you, too."

"I'm not in love," Marsh suddenly cautioned, as though fearful she might misconstrue his "caring."

"Oh, neither am I," she assured him, and at once knew that it was a lie. But what else could she say to a man who had to struggle to admit so simple a concept as caring?

He seemed relieved by that. "So we can begin again?"

"Begin what?" Annie gently questioned.

"Our relationship, I guess." He shrugged. "I don't know."

Annie considered his question in silence for a moment and quite seriously. Marsh's admission of affection was a big step forward. He'd been touched— something he'd said hadn't happened in a long time.

She found that vastly encouraging, and why not? Didn't it mean a relationship with Marsh would be a gamble, instead of a losing proposition?

It did . . . at least to Annie. Ever the optimist, she honestly believed that any man capable of missing someone was also capable of loving them.

And if he could learn to love, who knows what else he could learn to do? Why, someday . . . maybe . . . he might even be able to promise his tomorrows.

Head over heels in love with him, willing to wait a lifetime if that's what it took, Annie wanted those tomorrows.

"We can begin again," she said. She held out her arms to him, and with a sound very much like a sob, he slid over the cushion and into her embrace. She hugged him hard, relishing this newfound closeness, and knew that any wait would be worth the ultimate prize.

Several moments of companionable silence passed. Marsh didn't try to kiss or touch her. They simply held one another.

Then he loosened his embrace and slipped out of her arms. "I guess we'd better get back before we're missed." His voice was husky with emotion.

"Yes," she reluctantly agreed.

"You go on, then. I'll be along in a minute."

"Okay." Annie stood and walked to the door, where she paused and turned back to Marsh, now standing by the window, his gaze on the bonfire. "Are you okay?"

He cleared his throat. "Yeah." Then he laughed softly. "Emotionally draining, this caring stuff, huh?"

"Yes," Annie agreed with candor. "But worth it, Marsh. Definitely worth it."

He made no immediate response to that. And after a second or two of silence, Annie guessed he wasn't sure enough to agree. With a soft sigh of resignation and just a little disappointment, she turned and exited the room.

Then and only then did Marsh reply, "I know," whispered words that to Annie's ears were as warm and full of promise as a bridegroom's "I do."

On Tuesday, Marsh and Annie turned their counselor duties over to their co-workers, who'd planned a hike for the campers. Then the two of them drove to the hospital for Hal's knee surgery.

Their morning—spent in a stark waiting room—dragged, though in actuality the procedure didn't take so very long.

Finally Hal's doctor, a man named Reece Amos, appeared and talked to them about the surgery, done with the aid of a laser. He assured them that all torn cartilage had been trimmed away and ligament damage repaired.

In other words, Dr. Amos said with a laugh, Hal would be "up and at 'em" again in a matter of days. Clearly he knew Hal well. And Marsh wasn't a bit surprised when the Doc then began to reminisce about his experiences as a camper at Timbertop, not so many years ago.

After a hilarious conversation, Dr. Amos gave Marsh and Annie permission to visit with his beloved patient, but cautioned them not to stay too long.

They didn't, limiting themselves to a brief quarter hour—just long enough to convince themselves Hal really was going to be all right.

When Marsh laid eyes on the old man, he felt a rush of relief so strong he actually struggled to keep his emotions in check. Astonishing, that depth of feeling, and a miracle for which he knew who to thank— Annie.

Hair tumbling down around her shoulders, wide eyes twinkling, she was a sight to behold as she teased a smile from Hal. And Marsh wanted nothing more than to take her in his arms and hold her tight forever.

Forever? Well, maybe not that long…yet. But since the word didn't make his blood run cold as it once had, Marsh acknowledged the possibility that a forever—if shared with Annie—might someday hold honest appeal.

More important—and this was the miracle—Marsh recognized that he really didn't mind that possibility.

By the time they drove back to Timbertop, the campers had returned from their hike.

Marsh immediately reassumed his role as counselor and camp manager by hustling them all to the lake, where he lined them up and took the official, Week One, Camp Timbertop photograph.

He then gave all twenty-four, plus the much deserving counselors, a couple of hours free time, during which he followed them around and took more photos, these candid.

Working with black-and-white film, Marsh captured the curiosity, the joy, the mischief of childhood. And when he headed to Hal's basement later that afternoon to process the four rolls of film he'd taken, Marsh suspected he'd done some of his best work.

He knew it for sure not long after. Standing in the darkroom Hal provided so many years ago, Marsh watched the photos develop and knew they were good.

He saw little girls whispering together, their eyes alight with the intrigue of a shared secret. He saw little boys leaping off the boat dock into crystal-blue water. He saw a counselor catnapping; he saw a nosy but well-meaning old woman peeling apples for a pie.

And he saw Annie, just as she'd looked that first night in the chow hall. Though surrounded by her girls, she'd given him her undivided attention for a split second—long enough to capture it for eternity.

Her face glowed. Her smile teased. Her eyes shone with unmistakable love.

Was the love for him? Marsh wondered as he stared at the photo, amazed at just how far he'd come this past week.

Far enough to return her love? Marsh wondered next, rashly pushing aside the possibility that she might have been thinking of her girls and not of him when he'd snapped the photo.

He assessed his feelings and came to the conclusion that if not in love already, he was three-quarters of the way there. And at his present rate of falling, that meant he'd be lost forever by the end of the week.

Forever. That word again.

The one that used to set his teeth on edge, but now intrigued him.

Yes, he had come a long way, and he couldn't wait to find out what lay around the next bend in his journey.

Marsh showed Annie his photos that night after lights-out, all but the one of her, that is. If she noticed its absence, she did not comment, something for which he was grateful since he wasn't ready to admit that it now lay under his pillow.

"Does this mean you've decided to do your book on the faces of youth?" Seated across from him at a table in the chow hall, she examined a particularly adorable picture of Melissa and her precious dolly.

"I haven't talked to my publisher, but it's a possibility since we don't know when Hal will come back. I just thought it might be wise to have these to fall back on."

"They're wonderful, Marsh." She smiled.

"Thanks," he said, taking note of how that smile didn't quite reach her eyes. "Is something wrong?"

She shrugged. "I was just thinking about how sad these kids are going to be if Hal has to close Timbertop."

"It would be a great loss," Marsh agreed.

"It would be a disaster," Annie corrected. "That's why I think I'll go talk to Quentin Neal next week."

"Who?"

"Quentin Neal. He's an accountant and a former camper. I thought he might be able to give us some advice on how to go about getting a loan."

"Good idea," Marsh said, not for the first time experiencing a stab of guilt. He'd given Hal's financial state little thought thus far, probably because he knew what had to be done and was still too big a coward to do it.

Their talk turned to other things, and Annie seemed to cheer up somewhat. But Marsh sensed in her a sadness that shamed him since he had the means to end it forever.

The means? Probably. The guts? Not yet and maybe never, a realization that made Marsh wonder if he'd made so much progress after all.

Hal looked downright chipper when Annie and Marsh visited him after lunch on Wednesday. He chattered nonstop, giving them reports of his progress—namely walking up and down the hall with the aid of a therapist.

"I hope to be back at camp by the weekend," he exclaimed. "And with a little luck, I'll be able to take over management duties, so you—" he pointed to Marsh "—can get back to Atlanta and get on with your career."

Marsh blinked in surprise at that news. He'd expected Hal's recovery to take much longer and discovered he wasn't exactly wild about the idea of leaving Annie now that they'd come to an agreement about their relationship.

What that relationship entailed, exactly, he wasn't sure. And that, he thought, was the reason he wanted to hang around a bit longer.

Nonetheless, he grinned and congratulated Hal on his news. "Then I might make my deadline after all, huh?"

"Looks that way," Hal agreed, clearly pleased.

Somewhat disconcerted, Marsh glanced over at Annie. Like him, she smiled and nodded, seemingly thrilled by Hal's news. Did she bluff as he did, or was her happiness sincere?

"I can't wait to have you back," she murmured to Hal. "I've missed you a lot."

He smiled. "Thank you, honey. Hearing that does this old man good."

"I've missed you, too," Marsh said, an expression of feeling that visibly shocked Hal, though not as much as his next comment. "I love you, Pops."

"And I love you, son," Hal said, his eyes round with astonishment, wet with tears. He glanced from Marsh to Annie, then back to Marsh, obviously trying to figure out what had happened while he lay there in his hospital bed.

Marsh offered no explanations. He didn't trust his voice.

Annie offered none, either, but did give Hal a hug. "And do you love me?"

"You know I do."

"Good, 'cause I love you, too."

Hal laughed and again looked from one to the other. Marsh could almost hear the unasked questions, based, no doubt on Roth-type logic. If Annie and Marsh loved Hal and he loved them back, could Annie and Marsh possibly, then, love each other?

"We'd better be getting back to camp," Marsh said, as much to put an end to Hal's wondering as his own.

"Yeah," Annie agreed. "Those kids have probably tied Ginger and Shane to a tree by now."

Hal chuckled. "And there's no telling what they might have done to the other two counselors."

Annie tensed at that and glanced to Marsh, guilt written all over her face.

"We'll see you, Pops," Marsh promised, grabbing Annie's hand and hustling her out the door before she gave anything away.

In minutes they sped down the highway in his Jeep, headed back to camp. But when Marsh reached the gate to the property, he drove right on past.

"You missed the turn!" Annie exclaimed, craning her neck to get a view of the gate, disappearing around a curve behind them.

"We're making a little side trip," Marsh informed her.

"Oh." After a second's hesitation, she settled back in her seat, her eyes on the road ahead, her brow knitted in a frown.

Marsh didn't keep her wondering long, in no time turning onto a dirt road and halting his vehicle next to a back, seldom-used gate to Timbertop.

"I didn't know this was here," Annie commented.

"It's a well-kept secret," Marsh replied. "Don't want any runaway campers."

"As if they'd run away." Annie smiled. "Our campers are happy ones."

"They are that," he agreed as he slipped out of the Jeep. He walked over to the gate, unlocked and swung it open, then walked back to the vehicle to drive onto the property. "Unfortunately they are also a whole lot of work, the reason I brought you here. Annie Winslow, we're going on a hike, just the two of us."

"A hike's not work?" she asked, but she laughed.

"A hike's adventure...especially when there's a cave waiting at the end of it." Again he stepped out of the

Jeep, this time walking back to relock the gate. He then drove a few yards farther before parking under a shade tree. "Follow me," he instructed, motioning for her to get out of the vehicle. Annie did as requested, and the two of them began their trek to Marsh's cave.

The hike was not an easy one. This section of Hal's property had not been cleared of the brambles and bushes that grew in the wild. Annie found the terrain uneven and rocky, and on more than one occasion she was saved from a stumble by Marsh, who held on to her tightly.

"How far?" she asked after a good ten minute's worth of hard walking lay behind them.

"We're close," Marsh replied, an answer that proved to be true moments later when they topped a small rise and found themselves standing within spitting distance of a rock ridge. Beautifully striped in shades of rust and brown, the massive formation seemed to go on for miles. Annie marveled that she'd never seen it before, not to mention the cave that lay just to their right about ten yards away.

"Wow," she murmured, as usual awestruck by God's handiwork.

"Impressive, huh?" Marsh replied, then led her to the cave's opening. He walked straight into the narrow rock split, or would have if Annie hadn't dug in her heels.

"Is it safe?" she asked.

Marsh laughed. "Would pirates have hidden their treasure here if it weren't?"

"What are you talking about?"

"You mean you haven't heard the story about the band of pirates who slipped inland and buried their treasure right here at Timbertop?"

"No," Annie replied, adding, "And if I had, I wouldn't have believed it. We're miles away from the coastline." She eased past and peered into the gaping hole, then gasped when Marsh sneaked up behind, scooped her up and stepped boldly inside. "Put me down!" she demanded, wiggling. But he wouldn't.

Instead, he ducked his head and headed straight through the dark to a place he knew well, a place where the sun beamed in through a crack in the vaulted ceiling and a fresh-water spring bubbled clear and cold out of bare rock at their feet.

The moment they reached this inner sanctum, Marsh set Annie on her feet again. He walked to the spring—a small pool of sun-gilded water—and picked up a tin cup that lay on a bed of moss. After dipping it into the water, he handed it to Annie.

She hesitated fractionally, then put the cup to her lips and drank deeply. Her eyes widened with obvious pleasure. And when she handed the cup back to him, she smiled. "May I have another?"

Marsh grinned and nodded. "Good stuff, huh?"

"Wonderful stuff," Annie corrected, then drank again. When she finished, Marsh drank his fill, too. While he did that, Annie explored their surroundings, at first rather nervously, then with some enthusiasm. "How long have you known about this cave?"

"I stumbled onto it my sixth summer at Timbertop. I never told anyone, not even Hal."

"Do you come here often?"

"Only when I need to be alone."

"Mmm." Annie sat on a moss-cushioned ledge and patted the space next to her, clearly inviting Marsh to sit there, too. "Is that why you brought me here today?" she asked once he'd joined her. "So I'll have a place to hide if I need to be alone?"

"That's part of the reason," he said.

"What's the other part?" She'd tensed and looked as though she fully expected him to admit to having a sexual motivation. Was she still so unsure of him? he wondered, oddly hurt.

"I brought you here so you could enjoy the beauty, too."

"Oh." Still she studied his expression. Marsh never blinked under her scrutiny, and he knew the exact moment she began to believe his words. "T-thank you, Marsh."

"You're welcome," he replied, words as formal as his tone.

Annie gave him another long look, then got to her feet to kneel at the water's edge. "Have you ever photographed this pool? It would make a striking print."

"I don't think I want anyone else to know about it."

She laughed, a sound that echoed in the close quarters. "You wouldn't have to tell the location."

"True."

"So do it."

Marsh considered her request, then shook his head. "I'm not sure I can say this so it will make sense . . ."

Annie rose, joined him on the ledge and slipped her hand into his. "Please try."

"All right." He thought for a moment more, then forged ahead. "This cave is a precious gift from God to Marsh McGriffey. I'm not sure how He'd feel if I gave His gift away."

Obviously considering his words, Annie didn't speak for several seconds, during which time Marsh didn't move a muscle or take his eyes off her. Then she seemed to come to some sort of conclusion.

Leaning forward, she touched her lips to his in the briefest of kisses. "God has given us many gifts. Your artistic ability is one of yours. My healing skill is one of mine. What do you think these would be worth if we never gave them away?"

"Are you saying it's selfish of me to keep this place a secret?"

"No. I'm just saying that it wouldn't be wrong if you shared the serenity."

"Just as a rich man should share his money?"

Annie nodded with enthusiasm. "Exactly. And just as a teacher should share her knowledge. We've all been blessed with gifts we should give away, Marsh . . . our time, our energy, our—"

"Love?"

"Y-yes." She looked a bit disconcerted, but did manage another nod. "And if we keep them to ourselves, if we're stingy or maybe scared to risk rejection of our gift, we miss out."

"On what, Annie?"

"On a blessing," she told him, adding, "Does this make any sense at all? Do you understand what I'm saying?"

"It does, and I do," Marsh replied, words from the heart; words that would have been a lie less than a week ago.

Chapter Eight

They stayed in the cave almost an hour, then slowly walked back to the Jeep. Marsh didn't start the motor the moment they got into the vehicle, and when he didn't, Annie turned to him, wondering why.

"I almost hate to go back," he admitted, answering the question she had not yet verbalized.

"Are you tired of managing Timbertop?" she asked, suddenly remembering his comments to Hal earlier that day. Newfound closeness or not, Marsh still intended to leave Virginia as soon as their benefactor could handle the camp again. That's probably why he hadn't tried anything back in the cave, and that's probably why she'd found his behavior both endearingly noble and damned disappointing.

"Actually, I kind of like it, and I love the kids."

Good grief! It seemed Ms. Potter's lone wolf had been transformed into a man any woman would cherish . . . any woman except Annie Winslow, that is. She would never get to enjoy the fruits of her labor. At least not if he went back to Atlanta.

And he said he was going there soon—so soon that a restless desperation now gnawed at her good intentions and threatened the wisdom of her lifelong goals.

"So why do you hate to go back to Timbertop?" she persisted, hoping against hope his reluctance had something to do with her. Heaven knew she didn't want to go back just yet, either, a feeling that had little to do with the responsibilities waiting there and much to do with the ache deep inside her, an ache only Marsh could appease.

"Well, it is a little hectic."

"Mmm-hmm."

"And the two of us never have a minute alone."

"We're alone now, Marsh." She turned in the bucket seat to face him.

He nodded slowly. "That we are."

"And so far we haven't acted one bit differently than we would if all twenty-four campers surrounded us."

"That could be remedied." He, too, turned, but he didn't reach for her, instead searching her face as though to discern her intentions.

Annie made them crystal clear. "Please," she murmured, leaning forward to touch her lips to his.

In a heartbeat she found herself caught up in his strong embrace. Again and again, he kissed her—deep, wet kisses that did nothing to ease her aching need, instead intensifying it.

Hungering for him, Annie slipped off the seat and onto Marsh's lap. Since she never broke their kiss, that put them heart to heart, with Annie's legs doubled back under her and straddling his. Raising up on her knees, which buried into the soft seat on either side of his thighs, she pressed kisses to every inch of his face.

Marsh made the most of her preoccupation with that part of his anatomy to check out a part of hers. In one smooth motion, he caught the hem of her knit top in his hands and pushed it up under her arms. That maneuver exposed her bra. And after kissing every millimeter of her breasts not covered by the peach-tinted lace, Marsh performed another maneuver that completely exposed both to his eager lips.

Annie gasped when he unclasped the bra, then gasped again when his hot kisses seared her sensitive skin. With his tongue, he teased the rosy tips to pebble tautness. Sheer sexual thrill shimmied down her spine and centered deep inside, further intensifying her need for him.

"Ah, Marsh," she gasped. "Touch me, touch me."

He did, and right where she wanted. A firm touch that soothed even through the jeans she wore. A touch that promised pleasure beyond anything she'd ever imagined.

She touched him, too, then. A different sort of touch—virginal and perhaps a little tentative in spite of her burning need for completion. Caught up in her fears of his departure, desperate for a oneness that might never be again, Annie tried to pretend sexual experience.

But Marsh wasn't fooled.

To Annie's dismay, he caught her exploring hands in his and held them fast against his racing heart.

"Are you sure about this?"

"What?" Yanked so abruptly back to earth from paradise, Annie couldn't even assimilate the question.

"You're twenty-seven years old and this is your first time, Annie."

"Are you holding that against me?" Annie asked, sitting back, refastening and rearranging her clothes. It didn't take a fool to figure out there would be no trip to paradise this day.

"Of course not. I just...well... It's obvious you've been saving yourself for the right man."

"So?"

"So I'm not sure I'm him."

"I don't mind," Annie assured him, and placed a kiss on the cleft in his chin.

Marsh turned his head and swallowed hard. "You may not, but I do. I've changed this past week, thanks to you. I care, and because I do, I don't want you to have regrets."

Annie solemnly considered his words. Their on-again, off-again passion had to be frustrating for him, yet he'd put her needs first.

"Talk to me, Annie. Tell me what you're thinking."

"I'm thinking I've created a monster," she grumbled, words that made Marsh chuckle and considerably lightened a very tense moment. Annie slid off his lap and slipped into her own seat again. She rested her elbow on the open window and stared out of it, looking at but not really seeing the tall timbers growing all around.

Marsh did a little shifting of his own—straightening in the seat, dropping his head back on the headrest, closing his eyes. Via a sidelong glance, Annie took note of the pulse pounding in his neck. She saw that his hands trembled and that sweat beaded his brow.

Clearly he would need time to cool off before they returned to camp. For that matter, so would she.

"Thanks," she murmured, reaching over to pat his denim-covered thigh.

"Does that mean you're okay with this?" His troubled, dark-eyed gaze touched her soul.

"Not yet, but hopefully I will be sometime in this lifetime."

"A cold shower might speed up the process." His grin looked very natural and sexy as all get-out.

"They work?"

"So I hear."

"You've never had to take one before?"

"Can't say that I have," he admitted. "And that, Red, is the ultimate compliment. I've never cared enough to stop before now."

Though relations between them could have—even should have—been strained, Marsh and Annie talked like old friends during the short drive to Timbertop's front gate.

As a result, they were both remarkably cool and collected when he parked the Jeep, a good thing since they were immediately surrounded by several rambunctious, perceptive campers.

Marsh headed indoors to give Ms. Potter a report on Hal's condition. Annie followed the campers to the dorm, where they all washed up for dinner.

The rest of the evening passed uneventfully, except for a minor disagreement between Marsh's twins and two more of his charges, seven-year-old boys named Gordon and Mike. It seems Jerry and David had short-sheeted the bunks of the younger boys.

Marsh quickly corraled all concerned, of course, then led them in a brisk jog around the rim of the campsite. He didn't ask the campers who weren't involved, Bobby and Phil, to join in the run, but oddly enough they wanted to, so they did.

And so did Shane's boys. A foot race naturally evolved and lasted for a noisy hour. All the girls cheered them on. And when the races were over, Ms. Potter gave the winners an extra-huge slice of the pies she brought out and served—pies really intended for dinner the next night.

Twenty-four exhausted campers fell into their bunks that night. Two equally worn-out counselors and one very tired cook soon followed suit.

As for Annie and Marsh—they waited until all had turned in, then met behind the storage shed to bid each other good night. She noted that he looked marvelously relaxed and wondered at it since she was still wound tight as a spool of thread herself.

"You found time for that cold shower?" she asked, a teasing question, but one to which she wanted an answer.

"The running did the trick," he told her. "Great stress reliever. You ought to try it." That said, he kissed her full on the mouth, pivoted and jogged off into the night.

"Running, huh?" With a maybe-I'll-just-try-that shrug, Annie set off toward her own dorm, arriving there winded, weary and just as wired as ever.

So much for that, she thought, heading for the showers. While running might work for Marsh Mc-Griffey, it did nothing for Annie Winslow, who wanted him even more than the fact that she didn't want to take any darned ol' cold shower.

Thursday dawned bright and clear, a fact for which Marsh said a small prayer of thanks. It was much easier to handle twenty-four lively boys and girls out of doors than inside.

Since that morning's activities involved all the campers being together, Annie and Marsh decided to visit Hal before lunch instead of after. They wanted to get back to Timbertop in time to watch auditions for the talent show to be held on Friday night, and Annie had an appointment with the accountant at five o'clock.

Marsh enjoyed the twenty-minute ride to the hospital. He loved being alone with Annie, even though their necessarily platonic encounters always left him feeling a bit lost and very empty.

To his way of thinking, feeling anything was a miracle. And he marveled at the difference a few short days with Annie had made in his life.

The two of them found Hal in high spirits and full of plans for Timbertop. He talked nonstop for the first twenty minutes of their visit, not even noticing that they became more reserved the longer he chattered about the camp.

Clearly he didn't have a care in the world. Marsh was glad they had not shared the state of his finances with him. He hoped Annie obtained some helpful information from Quentin Neal before they were forced to tell Hal the truth.

Though Annie and Marsh had really planned to leave before lunch, Hal insisted that they eat with him down in the hospital cafeteria. They agreed, just to keep him happy, then wound up staying even later than that . . . three-thirty to be exact.

It seemed that Hal wanted them to meet someone at that particular time—a female someone named Esther Rose Millholland. One of the gracious volunteers who came daily to each room to brighten the patients' days. This silver-haired senior citizen positively lit up the room when she walked through the door bearing magazines and candy.

Instantly Marsh realized the reason for Hal's good mood—Ms. Esther Rose. Two minutes into her visit, he realized something else: Hal was well and truly smitten.

Good, he thought, a sentiment Annie shared if her twinkling eyes and wide smile were anything to go by.

The four of them had a nice conversation. Marsh even managed to slip quite a few casual, but important questions into it. Was Esther Rose a local? Was she married? Did she own a home? Drive a car?

Since all her answers were the right ones, Annie asked a few questions of her own—questions that revealed she was as big a romantic as she was an optimist.

What did Esther Rose think of Hal's owning a youth camp? How did she feel about country life? And, most important, did she like children?

Again all the answers were the right ones.

By the time Annie and Marsh left that afternoon at four o'clock, they knew just about everything they needed to know about Esther Rose except the size of her shoes and her bank account.

"It sure would be nice if she was rich," Annie murmured, words that earned her a look of censure from Marsh.

"For shame," he scolded.

"But we're desperate," Annie retorted.

"Desperate enough to sacrifice Hal? That would be defeating our purpose, don't you think?"

"Maybe," Annie replied, giggling like one of her campers when she added, "But he'd die a happy man."

Marsh could only agree and joined in her laughter. And though talk turned to other things, they were both still smiling by the time they pulled through Timbertop's gates.

The second Marsh halted his Jeep, Ginger ran up to it, wide-eyed and clearly distraught.

"Thank goodness you're back," she exclaimed when he opened the door. "We've lost the twins."

"Lost them? What do you mean, lost them?" Marsh as good as yelled.

"They've gone. Vanished. We've looked everywhere close, and Shane's out in the woods looking for them now. They simply are not to be found." She began to cry then, and instantly Marsh wished he hadn't been so loud.

So did Annie, who gave him a hard look and Ginger a big hug. "It's okay," she soothed the sobbing counselor. "Nobody's blaming you."

"But I was in charge."

"Of too many children," Marsh replied. "If this is anyone's fault, it's mine. Frankly, I think Jerry and David are to blame. They know better than this."

"Have you questioned the other children?" Annie asked, guiding Ginger away from the Jeep to where a huddle of campers waited. She saw that Ms. Potter was there, too, and all of them looked terribly worried.

"Yes, but if anyone knows anything, they're not telling."

"Maybe if I ask," Marsh murmured, striding ahead. In seconds, he'd gathered the ten boys around him—probably because they were more likely to know more than the girls, who had "cooties" and, therefore, weren't privy to male companionship or their secrets.

"All right, guys," he said. "Tell me what you know."

Dead silence followed his request.

"Aw, come on," he said. "Surely someone knows something."

Again there was silence.

"Do Jerry and David like camp?" asked Annie, who had walked up and now stood next to the circle of males.

"They hate it," replied Gordon.

"Yeah," agreed Bobby. "They think it's boring."

"They told you that?" murmured Annie, exchanging a glance with a frowning Marsh.

"Uh-huh," said Gordon. "Said they went to a really neat camp last year. One with horses and stuff."

"Where was that?" Annie next asked, wondering if the boys might have decided to switch camps or something.

"Down around Danville," interjected one of Shane's boys, a ten-year-old. "That's where they were living when their mom and dad got killed."

So Jerry and David were orphans. Annie had forgotten that.

At that moment, Marsh pulled her aside. "You keep asking questions. I'm going to look for the boys."

"God, I hope you find them," Annie said, her voice strained with worry.

Marsh took one look at her, then drew her into his arms for a quick hug. "Timbertop may be huge, but it's surrounded by a ten-foot chain-link fence with barbed wire on top of it. Odds are our missing campers are still within the confines of that fence. And if they are, Shane or I will find them. Nobody knows this place better than we do."

"Should I call the sheriff?" Annie asked, not so sure. As he'd said, Timbertop *was* huge. How could two men possibly search each and every inch of it?

"Good idea," Marsh told her.

Turning, he walked to the boy's dorm, pausing only long enough to say something to Ginger and then to Ms. Potter. He vanished into the building, reappearing a few moments later bearing a flashlight and a canteen.

With a wave, he disappeared into the trees, leaving Annie to deal with twenty-two hyperactive campers, a nearly hysterical counselor and a very worried cook.

She felt a brief moment of panic, but then her ER experience kicked in. In mere minutes, each and every camper had been assigned a task designed to keep them busy and in sight until dark. Surely Jerry and David would be back in camp, safe and sound, by then.

Annie next called the sheriff, whose deputies arrived within the hour, blue lights flashing. That, of course, caused quite a stir, and chaos once again prevailed.

The moment Ronnie White, the only one of the deputies Annie knew, stepped from his shiny white truck, he was surrounded by campers, all of whom blurted the problem and at the same time, some of whom then began to cry.

He never even blinked. Instead he somehow managed to quiet everyone, demonstrating skills he'd most likely learned while a counselor at this very camp.

"Well, if it isn't Annie Winslow!" he exclaimed when Annie made her way to the front of the crush. "Are you married yet?" Ronnie's unexpected query produced giggles from the girls and groans from the guys.

"As a matter of fact, I'm not," Annie told him, well aware that his teasing tone and flirty wink were intended to put the children at ease. "Why do you ask?"

Ronnie stuffed his hands into his pockets and scuffed the sandy ground with the toe of his shoe. "I've been thinking for some time about popping the question myself."

"And are you going to do it?" Annie noticed that every child—male and female—now watched Ronnie's antics with wide eyes, a sure indication that two lost boys were now the last thing on their young minds.

"I believe I just might," Ronnie drawled, an answer that produced a gasp from one of the girls. Turning, the deputy located the child in question—Diane. "You don't think I should ask Miss Annie to marry me?"

Diane shook her head quite vigorously.

"And just why not?" he demanded, walking over, dropping down onto one knee so that they were eye level with one another.

"Because she's going to marry Marsh." This time it was Annie who gasped, a sound lost in the commotion following Diane's reply.

"But if she marries him, who am I going to marry?"

"Ginger don't have no husband," Diane replied, pointing to the counselor in question.

General hilarity followed. When it died down, a scant five minutes after Ronnie's arrival at the camp, a crimson-cheeked Ginger, once more a functional counselor and very anxious to make an escape, was able to put them all to work again.

This, of course, left Annie free to explain the situation to Ronnie and the other deputy, which she quickly did.

The men listened to her tale, contacted their dispatcher, then headed into the woods, each with a hand-held radio for communication purposes—radios identical to the one left at the camp just in case they boys returned on their own.

Though Annie felt immensely better, she had trouble concentrating on the simplest of tasks. Finally she gave up and headed to the house proper, intending to hide in the parlor for just a few minutes.

She'd made it almost to the back door when someone came running up behind and tugged on the hem of her blouse.

"Miss Annie?"

She halted and turned. "What is it, Melissa?"

"I need to tell you something."

Annie tensed, suddenly remembering that Melissa and the missing twins came from the same orphanage. "You do?"

"Uh-huh."

"About David and Jerry?"

"Uh-huh."

"Do you know where they've gone?"

"Uh-huh."

"Where, honey? Tell me where they are."

"At the cave."

Annie frowned. "What cave?"

"The one with the treasure in it that the pirates left."

How on earth could those boys have heard that old tale? Annie wondered as she dropped to her knees to put herself eye level with Melissa.

"Where did they hear about this cave?"

"Lester told them."

Lester? Frantically, Annie searched through her brain, trying to figure out who he could be. She came up with nothing. "How did Lester know about it?"

"He found it last year. He drew a map. There's a big X where the pirate gold is.

"So that was it. Lester, probably one of last year's charity campers, had found the cave just as Marsh had. Unfortunately, he'd spilled his secret, embellishing it with a little pirate treasure nonsense.

"Why didn't you tell me this before?" Annie asked Melissa.

Her china blue eyes instantly filled with tears. "Jerry said he'd pull off Betsy's head and bury it in the woods."

"Betsy? Oh, your dolly." At once sympathetic, Annie gave Melissa a big hug and a kiss. She, of all people, knew just how precious keepsakes could be to an orphan.

She also knew the way to that old cave.

"Nobody's going to hurt Betsy, Melissa. I won't let them." That said, Annie turned the child back toward the others and gave her a little push on the tush. "Thanks for helping us find the boys. Now you go on back, okay?"

Melissa nodded and, clearly feeling better, ran back to her friends.

Glancing at her watch, Annie noted the time: five forty-five. It would not be dark for a long time, though that didn't really make a difference. That cave wasn't but ten minutes away if one approached it from the back of camp.

Anxious to find the boys and end this little escapade, Annie ran to Ms. Potter and told the woman where she was headed. She then hopped in her car and headed out the gate. Unlike Marsh, she took no flashlight with her. What would she need one for?

She and the boys would be back long before dark.

Chapter Nine

Deep in the beautiful woods of Timbertop, Marsh glanced at his watch. Six o'clock. He still had a couple hours of daylight left.

Good.

Though he'd been able to utilize his military skills in tracking the boys this far, the trail was not as clear as he had expected, and the going was frustratingly slow.

As Marsh walked, methodically scanning the rocky ground beneath his feet and the undergrowth on all sides of him, he thought about Hal, about Annie and about Timbertop.

Both Hal and Annie would be heartbroken if anything happened to the place. Marsh, himself, would miss it, too, more proof that he'd come a long way in the past week.

Far enough to pay an overdue visit to his grandparents and request a loan? Marsh wondered. He seriously considered the idea, trying to picture himself at his grandparents' stately mansion, sipping tea in the parlor or seated at their mile-long dinner table.

His skin crawled as some unpleasant memories washed over him. He flatly nixed the idea of a homecoming.

This week with Annie had mellowed him, there was no denying that. But not enough to humble himself to his granddad, it seemed.

Besides, Annie and Hal would rightly expect more than just money from him. They would expect his time and energy. They would expect commitment. Marsh searched his soul and knew he wasn't capable of giving that yet.

Sadly, he wondered if he'd ever be.

Suddenly Marsh heard a sound that wasn't quite in tune with nature. He stopped short, cocked his head and stood in absolute stillness, listening.

Sure enough, he'd heard voices, Marsh realized in seconds. They sounded far away and to his right. He couldn't tell if they were distressed.

For that reason he proceeded in their direction as stealthily as possible. Oh so quietly through the dense undergrowth he slipped, his ears attuned to the very human sounds clearly emanating from just over a small rise.

Minutes later he topped that rise, ducking when he spied Timbertop's lost boys, both of whom kneeled down on the dirt and stared at a large piece of paper lying on the ground before them.

Curious, Marsh did not reveal his presence right away. From all appearances, the boys were having the time of their life. And though they'd acted with utter irresponsibility and certainly deserved punishment, he was loathe to end their little adventure.

How many more chances would they have to be this free before the responsibilities of making a living shackled them?

"We're going the wrong way," said Jerry. At least Marsh guessed it was Jerry. The boys were identical twins and did have their backs to him.

"We are not."

"Are, too."

"Are not!"

Marsh almost laughed. Now that was a constructive conversation if ever he'd heard one.

"Lester said that cave was east of camp. Look at the sun. We're way west."

Lester? Cave?

David stood and tried to find the sun, but had no success—not surprising since the trees formed a canopy overhead and the sun now sank low on the horizon.

"I don't see no sun."

Jerry snorted his disgust. "It's over here...uh, wait...maybe it's over there."

"Are we lost?" David demanded, his voice edged with nervousness. Marsh almost stepped into view then, but waited.

"We ain't lost. We have a map."

"But it don't make no sense."

Jerry stood and looked his brother in the eye. "Reckon Lester was fooling us?"

David shrugged. "He said he wasn't, and he did have that gold piece...."

"Yeah, but we're awfully far away from water. How'd them pirates lug that old chest this far? It had to be heavy."

Pirates? Chest? Those boys had believed that old tale?

Marsh shook his head, amazed—until he remembered he'd once believed it, too.

"I wanna go back."

"You sure?" Jerry asked.

David nodded. "Yeah."

"They'll probably skin our hides."

"So what? We'll get to eat supper."

"What was Ms. P. cooking for tonight, anyway?"

"Catfish, fried potatoes, hush puppies and peach cobbler."

"Peach cobbler?"

"Yeah. I saw her peeling them this morning."

"Maybe we should go back. I wouldn't want anyone to worry about us."

"Nah."

Jerry looked all around. "So which way do we go?"

David did the same, then pointed north—the exact wrong way.

"Hello, there, boys," Marsh exclaimed, wisely choosing that moment to step into full view. "Where're you two headed?"

Eyes wide as cupcakes, faces white as cotton, the boys eyed him as though he were the ghost of one of those pirates they'd heard about.

Jerry cleared his throat. "Um, hello, um, sir."

Sir? Marsh almost choked. "Hello, yourself, son."

"We were just heading back to camp." David pointed off to the north again.

"That so?"

"Yes, sir."

"Hmm. Well, I hate to be the one to tell you fellas this, but that's not the way back to camp."

"It ain't?"

"No."

Jerry and David exchanged a look. "Which way is?" David asked.

"That way." Marsh pointed to the south.

"Oh." Again the boys exchanged a look.

"I just happen to be headed back, myself," Marsh said. "Do you guys want to come along?"

Both nodded vigorously.

"Fine, then, and on the way back let's have us a little talk, okay?"

For the third time Jerry and David exchanged a look, this one mutually guilty. "Okay."

So the three of them set off and arrived at camp around seven-thirty. The sun had set completely by then, leaving the sky dusky dark, but still light enough that someone spotted their approach long before they burst through the trees into the clearing.

As a result, Marsh and the boys found themselves surrounded by cheering, bouncing campers, all of whom seemed ecstatic to have them safely back. Jerry and David obviously enjoyed the attention, but the minute they began to get cocky, Marsh put them firmly in place by reminding them they owed their counselors—including Shane, now back at camp, himself—and their fellow campers a big apology.

Each boy gave that apology; then each stated what they had learned from their misadventure.

Jerry went first. "I learned, um, that it's not nice to, um, scare your counselors by leaving without telling them."

"Or your cook, either," interjected Ms. Potter, reaching out to affectionately ruffle his hair.

Jerry blushed, but grinned.

"David?" Marsh prompted.

The child in question thought for a moment. "I learned it's great to be on your own sometimes, but mostly it's better to be with your friends."

Everyone laughed and agreed with that—everyone except Marsh. Oh, he agreed, all right, but he didn't laugh. In his opinion, no truer words had ever been spoken.

And this youthful insight into life and living stayed heavy on his mind all during dinner, which was shared with the deputies called back into camp via the radio left there.

Marsh didn't have a moment to himself during the noisy meal. They didn't eat in the chow hall as usual, instead picnicking right out in the middle of camp. For that reason, Marsh was not concerned when on two different occasions he scanned the crowd for Annie and did not immediately find her.

She was around somewhere, he knew. Probably helping Ms. Potter with the plates, or maybe in the big house calling Quentin Neal to explain why she'd missed her appointment with him.

The thought of her meeting with Quentin made Marsh squirm with guilt. Maybe he needed to rethink his decision not to go to his grandparents for help.

Maybe he did . . .

"Yo, Marsh."

Marsh started, then grinned at the deputy gripping his shoulder. "Ronnie! Good to see you." He nodded toward a nearby camp chair that no one presently occupied. "Have a seat."

"I can't stay," Ronnie replied. He glanced toward his truck, in which his fellow deputy already sat. "We've had another call."

"Did you two get plenty to eat?"

Ronnie nodded and patted his stomach. "Ms. P. hasn't lost her touch, has she?"

Marsh laughed. "No." He stood, then, and extended his right hand. "Thanks for your help today."

Ronnie took, shook and released the proffered hand. "No problem. Call us anytime."

"Thanks."

"We'll see you soon," Ronnie said, moving away. "Be sure and invite me to the wedding."

"What wedding?" Marsh asked.

Ronnie grinned. "Yours and Annie's, of course."

"Mine and . . . Who in the world told you that Annie and I were getting married?"

Ronnie turned and scanned the scattered campers, then pointed to one of Annie's girls.

"Now why would she say a thing like that?" Marsh mused aloud.

"You mean, it's not true?" Something in Ronnie's tone of voice gave Marsh pause, and he quickly perused the other man's expression.

He saw speculation; he saw hope; he saw desire for Annie.

"We just haven't announced it yet," Marsh finally answered, words that were not a lie...exactly.

Ronnie chuckled. "Kids are darned perceptive, aren't they?" Clearly he believed that Annie and Marsh had plans.

"Aren't they?" Marsh smoothly agreed without an ounce of remorse.

Ronnie left shortly after that. Once again, Marsh looked around for Annie, but still found no sight of her. Now a bit concerned, he glanced at his watch: eight-fifteen.

He peered up at the sky: dark.

He strode over to the nearest camper, Phil.

"Have you seen Miss Annie?"

"Not for a while," the boy replied around a bite of peach cobbler.

Marsh frowned and asked another child...then another. No one had seen Annie "for a while" it seemed. And by the time he reached Ms. Potter, his heart had begun to thump with fear.

"Have you seen Annie, Ms. P.?" he asked the older woman, who bustled about refilling cobbler bowls.

"Not for a—" At once her eyes rounded. "Oh, my goodness!"

"Where is she?" Marsh demanded, instantly attuned to Ms. Potter's distress.

"I'm not sure. She said something about going to a cave in the back forty to look for the boys, then left in her car."

"Damn!" Marsh muttered, turning on his heel, jogging to his Jeep. He paused only long enough to snatch up a flashlight, then leapt into the vehicle and exited camp with a spray of gravel and dirt.

Driving much faster than was safe, Marsh reached the back exit in record time. There he found Annie's car, parked outside the locked fence. A tiny piece of cloth caught on the barbed wire that topped the tall fence told him that Annie had climbed over to get inside. Amazing, Marsh thought, unlocking the gate, slipping through it on foot.

At a dead run, he crossed the clearing, where, he slowed to a walk and plunged into the dense woods.

With only the beam of a flashlight to guide him, Marsh headed steadily toward the cave. Progress was slow. He didn't want to miss any track, any broken twig that might show him the way to Annie—the woman he loved.

That he loved her, Marsh suddenly had no doubt. How long he'd loved her, he didn't know. The emotion could have been so gradual, it took a knock on the head such as this for him to recognize it. Or perhaps it was an all-at-once sort of thing, a blinding flash of insight and realization.

Whatever... he was in love, and he found he didn't mind it one damn bit.

So what now? he asked himself as he crashed deeper and deeper into the forest.

Nothing, he realized, until he found her. If he found her.

"I'll find her," Marsh growled, and then, to make sure, began to bargain with God.

Let her be safe, Marsh promised Him, and I'll cancel my subscription to *Stud* magazine. Let her be safe, and I'll never drink another beer. Let her be safe, and I'll get that loan to save Timbertop. Let her be safe, and I'll marry her.

Yes, marry her. He was that far gone.

The minutes ticked by and still Marsh pushed ahead. He developed a sort of pattern: light straight ahead so he could memorize the terrain, light to the left and then right to look for Annie.

Light straight ahead—he saw brambles, bushes, trees and vines.

Light to the left—nothing but more of the same.

Light to the right—

Marsh stumbled and fell . . . hard.

"Oomph!" exclaimed someone—Annie—over whose leg he'd tripped. Sitting under a tree a little to his right, she immediately pounced on the man lying prone over her legs. "Marsh!"

He was up on his knees in an instant, yanking her into his arms, holding her so tight.

"Oh, thank God," he breathed, words not nearly so loud as the pounding of his heart. "Are you okay?"

"Yes."

Marsh reached for the flashlight he'd dropped and shone it in her face, as though to verify for himself.

Annie blinked and pushed it aside. "I'm all right, Marsh. Really."

"Then why are you sitting here?" he demanded, sitting down. That move put his backside on the ground and Annie on his lap. "I've been scared out of my mind."

"I was waiting for the moon to rise so I could find my way back to the car. I don't have a flashlight." She picked a dead leaf off his shirt. "Tell me you found the boys."

"Yeah. Hours ago."

"What did you do to them?" she asked.

"Not nearly as much as I'd like to do to you," he retorted. "What were you thinking of coming out here by yourself without a flashlight?"

"It was early. I figured I'd just drive down here and get them. They were headed to the cave, you know."

"I know." He drew in a shuddering breath. "You'd only been here once before, Annie. You should have known you'd get lost."

"I'm not lost."

"Right."

Annie scrambled to her feet and glared down at him. "I am not lost!"

Marsh sighed wearily, stood and looked down at his precious, precious redhead. "Have I told you lately that I love you?"

"What?" Annie sat back down on the ground with a soft plop.

"I love you," Marsh repeated, handing her the flashlight, reaching for her, lifting her up into his arms. Turning, he began the long trek back to their vehicles. "Light the way, honey."

At that gentle reminder, Annie directed the beam so that Marsh could see where to step.

"I love you, too, Marsh," she then whispered.

He stopped at once and kissed her full on the mouth—a kiss that mattered more to him than any other they'd shared because this time it really meant something.

"Do you honestly think you can carry me all the way back to the gate?" Annie asked when Marsh began to walk again.

"Sure. The old adrenaline's really pumping…" He laughed. "In fact, I could probably carry you clear back to camp." And over the nearest threshold.

Though tempted to drop to his knees again—this time to propose, as promised—Marsh didn't go that far. There were other promises to keep first and, besides, Annie didn't need another shock this day.

Within the hour, they drove back through the front gates of the camp, Annie in the lead. Their campers, counselors and cook greeted them warmly, and Jerry and David were so glad to see "Miss Annie" that they actually offered an apology without being reminded.

Though everyone wanted to hear what had happened, Marsh somehow managed to hold them all at bay while Annie gulped down a few bites of dinner.

More than once during that short meal, she caught him looking at her with an expression she could not quite read. And more than once, he started to say something, then caught himself.

Guessing he wasn't exactly sure how to act now that they had professed their love—something that was bound to be difficult for a man so inexperienced in relationships as he—Annie tried to put him at his ease. "All our problems are solved, Marsh. Everything is going to be just perfect from now on."

Marsh opened his mouth to reply, but never had a chance before Annie's six girls lost patience and descended on her. They had a surprise for Miss Annie, they said. She should go with them to the dorm, now!

Bone weary, Annie gave Marsh a see-ya-later smile and let her campers lead her there. And though she would have loved nothing better than to be left alone to assimilate the miracle of Marsh's love, she let her solicitous girls pamper her—their "surprise."

First, Diane gently combed Annie's tangled hair. When that was accomplished, Jonni smeared night cream on Annie's face. Following that, Judy and Glenda rubbed lotion on Annie's hands, after which Patricia told Annie a bedtime story. Last, but not least, Melissa loaned her doll Betsy to Annie, then tucked them both in.

The girls, themselves, crawled into their bunks shortly after. And lying in the dark, surrounded by the sounds of their sleep, Annie said a little prayer of thanks for the gift of their love.

She thought about her life and realized just how many times she had been given that gift—her parents while she had them, all her foster parents while she had them, Hal, Opal, Marsh.

Precious Marsh.

Be smart with your heart. That familiar voice echoed in her head, so loudly that she opened her eyes and actually glanced around, seeing nothing, of course.

"But he loves me," she whispered back, confused to be hearing such advice now that Marsh had declared his feelings. Surely her heart could be in no danger if he loved her. Why, their future was as bright as a rising sun.

They would marry, have the children she'd always wanted, grow old together...or so Annie had assumed. Now that she really thought about it, Marsh hadn't said one word about a wedding.

But he would. Oh, yes, he would.

"Be smart with my heart?" She grinned. "You betcha!"

* * *

When Annie opened her eyes on Friday morning, she took one good look around and knew that things were back to normal. To her left, two girls fought over a hairbrush that belonged to neither. To her right, two more pored over a smuggled-in tabloid. And at the foot of her bottom bunk, Melissa smashed a bug with Annie's favorite slipper.

Ah, the joys of Timbertop!

Eager to lay eyes on Marsh—what if yesterday were a dream?—Annie leapt from her bed, performed an abbreviated toilette, then dashed to the chow hall for breakfast.

But he wasn't there.

"Shane, have you seen Marsh?" Annie asked the sleepy-eyed counselor, trying to halt a food fight.

"He left camp over an hour ago," Shane replied. "Said he would try to be back in time for the talent show tonight."

He'd left the camp? "Did he seem all right?"

"Yeah, sure." Shane shrugged and looked away, in Annie's opinion not so sure about that.

And suddenly, she wasn't, either. Where on earth had Marsh gone so early? More important, why hadn't he told her he was leaving? Surely he must have known how anxious she'd be to see him today. Surely he wanted to see her, too....

But what if he hadn't wanted to see her? she suddenly wondered. What if he'd had second thoughts about their relationship?

He'd changed so fast from loner into lover. Had it been too much, too soon? Was he now worried that she would expect more than he could give? Did he feel trapped in her hopes and dreams?

Be smart with your heart.

There it was again!

But this time when Annie heard that voice of gloom and doom, her blood ran cold.

Pivoting, she left the chow hall at a fast walk and then ran to the big house. Taking the stairs two at a time, she dashed to Marsh's room.

On hasty inspection, the area looked empty of his things. Annie caught her breath, at once certain he'd lied to Shane and gone for good. Baffled, she walked over to sit on the bed, only to trip over a black leather bag of some sort. She bent down to examine it closer.

His camera case.

"Oh, thank goodness!" Annie exclaimed, hugging that precious case to her chest, prancing around the room like an Indian at a rain dance.

He was coming back. Marsh was really coming back.

Everything was going to be okay.

She headed back downstairs then, and reassumed her counselor duties—duties that kept her busy until after lunch. Annie kept one eye on the gate the whole time, fully expecting to see Marsh drive through it at any moment.

He never did.

The one o'clock talent show was a riot—or should have been. As she had all morning, Annie kept one eye on the gate, watching for the man she loved to come home.

He never came.

And because he didn't, Annie did something she thought she wouldn't have to do—head back to the big house to call Quentin Neal for another appointment. Unfortunately, the phone was dead, as common an occurrence in their neck of the woods as power failures and one about which she didn't give a second thought.

Instead, vowing to call her friend from Hal's hospital room, Annie headed to town alone to see Hal.

"Where's Marsh?" the old man asked the moment she walked into his room alone at three o'clock.

"I don't know," Annie had to answer, unwilling to lie. Secure in her hopes that Marsh would come through for them, she had kept too much from Hal that week.

So with carefully chosen words, she told him everything she knew about Marsh's disappearance, about the state of Hal's finances, about her appointment with the accountant the first of next week.

Hal nodded as if he received such bad news every day, then offered possible reasons why Marsh might have left them so abruptly and without explanation— reasons she would've thought likely that very morning. Reasons she now could not accept so easily.

In spite of his show of confidence, it was obvious Hal was hurt. Precious Hal. And though he didn't complain, Annie's heart ached for him even more than for herself.

Chapter Ten

Marsh halted his freshly washed Jeep in front of his grandparents' Charlottesville home and killed the engine. With some reluctance, he glanced toward the stately mansion.

It looked the same as it had the last time he saw it, fifteen years ago—probably the reason his palms began to sweat.

With a shiver of pure apprehension, Marsh glanced at his watch: five minutes before four o'clock. Thanks to some highway repairs just out of Roanoke, he was much later than he'd meant to be. In fact, he'd missed the talent show back at Timbertop, darn the luck, but he was right on time for his appointment with his grandparents—an appointment that was a last-minute idea and made through their social secretary only an hour before.

What did said relatives think about this appointment? Marsh wondered as he made his way up the multitude of steps onto the porch. Were they angry? Curious? Resentful? Marsh didn't have a clue, so he rang the bell with a trembling hand.

Almost instantly, a pretty young woman opened it. He did not recognize her.

"Marsh McGriffey," he said, his voice a nervous croak. Marsh cleared his throat. "I have an appointment."

"Oh, yes. Come in," she said, stepping back so he could.

They walked together across a parquet entranceway, then down a hall. Marsh looked all around, noting that little had changed—or had it?

What had once seemed a mile-long hallway was really rather short, and the decor of the house didn't look nearly so austere as he remembered, either.

"Right in here," said the woman, reaching to open a door. "Your grandparents are expecting you."

With a nod, Marsh slipped past her and into a room he knew was his grandfather's study. He expected dark drapes and floors, walls that closed in. Instead he found a pleasant room—light, airy, warm.

"Marshal! What a nice surprise!" Clayton Cassidy rose and walked over to him, extending his right hand in welcome.

Marsh took and shook it. "Grandfather." He nodded to the woman still seated on the couch. "Grandmother."

"Hello, Marshal. It's been a long time."

It has, indeed, he silently replied, anxiously scanning Marissa Cassidy's expression. He saw curiosity, which he'd expected; he saw nervousness, which he had not.

"Too long," Marsh murmured, and found that he actually meant it. Funny that he hadn't realized that before now.

"Sit down, sit down." Clayton released Marsh's hand and directed him to a chair across from the couch, on which the old man then sat next to his wife.

Seated across from them, the object of their undivided attention and unspoken speculation, Marsh felt a bit like a man on trial for past crimes—probably not such an outrageous comparison now that he thought about it.

"I guess you two are wondering why I'm here."

"We are a bit curious," Marissa admitted. "We haven't heard one word from you in over fifteen years, after all. Not one word."

"Marissa." Clayton said his wife's name softly, but Marsh heard the censure.

"It's okay. She has a right to be angry with me. So do you." He drew in a shaky breath. "I owe you both an apology, and that's actually one of the reasons I'm here."

Suddenly unable to sit still, Marsh stood and walked over to the mantel. Absently he examined the treasures dotting it: a Fabergé egg, a Waterford clock, a picture of his mother.

Marsh's heart slammed into his rib cage.

Abruptly he abandoned his exploring and turned back to his patiently waiting grandparents.

"I'm not exactly sure how to say this... I mean, it isn't easy admitting that I've been a rebellious, ungrateful jerk for the past thirty-one years. But I have, and I want you two to know that I realize it now, and I'm sorry."

His grandparents exchanged a look, but said nothing.

"I also want to thank both of you for all you've done for me—the nannies, the clothes, the cars, the schools. I was one lucky kid to have you two step in when Mama died. I realize that now, too, and I want to be sure you know how much I appreciate your taking your responsibilities toward me so seriously."

Again his grandparents shared a glance, but this time his grandfather spoke. "It was our duty, yes, but we wanted to do it."

"Yeah, well, thanks," Marsh murmured, seriously doubting the truth of Clayton's words.

"We loved your mother, Marshal," Marissa said, as though reading Marsh's mind. "We could have helped her as much as we helped you, but she just wouldn't let us."

"Maybe her independence was more important to her than material wealth," Marsh said, the next instant wishing he hadn't been so candid. The bridge he now built was a delicate one and only partway complete. One false move might send it crashing into the river of self-exile that had kept them apart for so long.

"Is that why you turned down my offer to back your career?" Clayton asked. "Because your independence was so important to you?"

"That, and pride," Marsh admitted, again with candor. "I thought that if I didn't take your money, I wouldn't have to admit I'd inherited my photography talent from you."

"I have all your books," Clayton said after an audible gulp. "There's your latest, over there." He pointed to the end of the mantel opposite Marsh's mother's photograph. "You're very talented—far more than I ever was."

"Thanks," Marsh replied, marveling at both the compliment and the placement of his book. He also marveled at the fact that the three of them could hold so normal a conversation. He didn't know exactly what he'd expected, but it wasn't this calm, honest chat. Could it be they constructed the bridge from their side of the river? Could it be they would all meet in the middle?

"Are you working on another?" Marissa asked. Marsh noted how slender she still was and how elegant, dressed in her navy blue pants and that sheer white blouse. Her large brown eyes reminded him of his mother's, just as Clayton's dark complexion did.

"As a matter of fact, I am," Marsh admitted. "I've been out at Timbertop this week—"

"It's still open?" Clayton asked.

"Barely. I'm helping out while Hal Roth's been laid up with a bad knee. I've photographed the children." He smiled. "Their faces are so—" He searched for the word.

"Open?"

"Exactly. I thought I'd collect photographs all summer, then put the best in a collection."

"You could call it 'Summer Camp,'" Marissa suggested.

"Or maybe 'Hello Mudder, Hello Fodder,'" Clayton interjected, a twinkle in his eye.

Reminded of the old Camp Granada song he hadn't heard in years, Marsh laughed aloud at his grandfather's little joke. To his delight, his grandparents laughed, too.

"I can't wait to see the pictures," Clayton then commented. "You do have a way with a lens."

Highly flattered by the praise, Marsh shrugged. "I have some of the snapshots with me. Would you like to look at them?"

"I would," Clayton said. "And I'd also like for you to stay for dinner." He glanced at Marissa. "Don't you think we have enough for one more mouth?"

"We have enough for several more. Why don't I call Stephanie and James. I know they would love to see Marsh."

"Oh, I can't stay that long," Marsh said, not quite sure he was ready to face his aunt and uncle. "I was due back at camp hours ago. They'll be worried."

"Couldn't you give them a call?" asked Marissa, with obvious disappointment. "We haven't seen you in so long...."

She was right, of course, so with a mental groan, Marsh gave in. "Where's the phone?"

"Over there. I'll go tell Cook."

But when Marsh tried to call Timbertop, he couldn't get through. Used to the quirks of rural telephone lines, he just shrugged that off, vowed to try again, and headed to his Jeep for the photos.

Though anxious to get back to camp to talk with Annie, who'd still been asleep that morning when he left, Marsh knew he had to stay a while longer in Charlottesville. Conscience demanded it.

Besides, sharing the photographs of the campers would be a good lead-in to a candid discussion regarding Timbertop's current problems. And maybe, God willing, he'd find strength to overcome the last of his foolish pride so he could ask his granddad for the loan.

Annie didn't turn in until midnight on Friday. Worried, and depressed, she paced Miss Opal's parlor and watched the road, jumping nervously when Paula and her brother, Harley, surprised her by pulling into the drive.

After introductions and a hug of sympathy, Annie gratefully directed them to their dorms so they could assume their duties as counselors. She then returned to the parlor, where she checked the telephone to see if it was working. For the first time that evening, she heard a dial tone and quickly hung up the receiver, certain that Marsh would now call.

But he never did.

Saturday morning, Annie leapt from the couch where she had slept and dashed to the window, hoping against hope that Marsh had slipped back to camp sometime during the night.

There was no Jeep in the drive, however, and so no Marsh in the chow hall when she met her girls there for a last official meal.

Heartbroken, fearful she would never see Marsh again, Annie glanced over to Shane, who caught her eye and shook his head. Clearly the counselor didn't know any more about Marsh's mysterious disappearance than she did. Neither did any of the campers—

male or female—or Ms. Potter, all of whom she had questioned at various times the day before.

Since all but five campers left Timbertop by noon that day, Annie felt free to seek some much-needed solitude before she had to drive to town to fetch Hal. She headed straight for the woods, of course, a tried and true source of serenity and joy.

But today the trees were just trees and the creek nothing more than a narrow ribbon of water. Nothing special about the woods anymore, she realized, and was not a bit surprised.

Annie always suspected Marsh was the reason that she smiled every time she thought of Timbertop. Now she knew.

He was the magic, and even if she and Hal found the money to save Timbertop, even if they kept the camp running for years to come, it would never be the same again.

Sighing gloomily, Annie gave up on her search for peace of mind. She walked back to camp, halting abruptly when she drew even with the door of the now-empty boys' dorm. On impulse, Annie walked inside and looked around. She saw a pile of lost-and-found clothing lying on the floor; an assortment of life jackets and fishing poles stashed in a corner; bunks, all stripped of their bedding except for one.

With a gasp of realization, Annie crossed over to that bottom bunk and sat on it. She picked up the pillow and sniffed—it *was* Marsh's—and then spied something—a face-down photograph where that pillow had laid. Curious, she picked up the photo, turned it over and saw . . . herself.

Instantly, Annie's eyes filled with tears she could not contain. Hoping none of the boys who were left would stumble back into the dorm in search of their lost things, she sat on Marsh's bunk and cried for all she had lost.

Her goals were insignificant when compared to the joy that could have been hers had she not tried to force them on Marsh. Why, even when they were closest physically—that afternoon in his Jeep near the cave—she hadn't been thinking compromise.

No, indeed. She had believed their close encounter would lead to love, and love to the commitment that would result in the husband, children and home she'd always wanted.

Poor Marsh. No wonder he'd called a halt to their lovemaking. And no wonder he'd felt the need to run away. Her love trapped him. And lone wolf that he was and always would be, he reacted by breaking free.

So what now? she wondered. Forget him?

Fat chance.

Annie wasn't even surprised to hear the voice today. "Then what do you suggest?"

Wait.

"But we're wasting time," Annie argued, placing the picture back under the pillow and ducking out of the bunk. "Why, I could sit here at Timbertop for years waiting on that man."

Look out the window, Annie. You won't have to wait that long.

Whirling, Annie did just that and saw Marsh's bright red Jeep, just pulling into the drive. With a squeal that was one part delight and three parts sheer relief, Annie raced from the dorm and straight to his waiting arms.

They hugged long and hard, but didn't kiss, watched as they were by the leftover campers, four counselors and Ms. Potter, all of whom had walked over at the sound of the approaching vehicle.

"Where have you been?" Annie demanded the moment Marsh set her on her feet again.

"Getting this," he replied, and handed her a check for an amazing amount of money.

"You've been with your grandparents all this time?"

"Yeah," he told her, adding, "I tried all night to call you. The phones were out."

"Only until midnight," she told him.

"You were up that late?"

Annie nodded. "Pacing ... worrying."

Marsh winced. "About me?"

"Of course, about you," Annie scolded. "I've been out of my mind, Marsh. I was afraid I'd never see you again."

"Oh, Annie." The words came out on a sigh. "How could you think for one minute that I would leave for good?"

"What else was I supposed to think?" she exclaimed, now oblivious to their witnesses. "You leave with no explanation, you're gone all day...." In her agitation, she flailed her arms and tossed her hair.

"Annie."

"And then this morning, when you still weren't back..."

"Annie."

"And still hadn't called ..."

"Annie!"

That near shout got her attention. "What?"

"Will you just be quiet for a minute? There's something I have to ask."

To Annie's astonishment, Marsh took her hand in his, then dropped to his knee right there in the dirt.

"Annie Winslow, will you marry me?"

Annie, now in shock, didn't even hear Ms. Potter's "I knew it!" much less the "Do it, Annie," the "Say yes," and the "Marry him," offered by their delighted witnesses.

What if he asked for her hand out of respect for her goals? she worried. "But you told me you preferred to fly solo."

"I said that?"

He sounded so surprised that Annie searched his expression. She saw joy. She saw love. She saw forever after—not hers, not his, but theirs—the one they were going to share.

At once sure of him and sorely tempted to blurt the answer he so obviously waited to hear, Annie simply cocked her head and countered with a question of her own.

"And just why should I marry you, Marsh McGriffey?" she asked, wondering if he would remember the right answer.

"Because if you don't, who will?" he instantly replied with a grin, adding, "Say it, Annie. Say yes."

He'll make you happy, don't you think?

"Yes, oh, yes!" Annie replied, words from the heart, words that earned her Marsh's smile, bright at their tomorrows.

Epilogue

The sound of the wind rustling the autumn leaves drew Hal Roth to his window. Looking out, he inspected his beloved Timbertop, now in the process of major renovation.

He saw carpenters, he saw roofers, he saw painters.

He saw electricians, he saw plumbers, he saw masons.

In short, he saw a miracle.

He closed his eyes on the busy sight and pictured Opal, the woman whose love and guidance had first made Timbertop a reality. She was probably watching, he thought. Probably smiling, too.

"Marsh!"

Grinning, Hal leaned forward to find the source of that familiar voice, one Annie McGriffey. Walking up to her was her husband, Marsh, and witnessing their loving kiss, Hal remembered another time he'd spied on them.

He'd suspected then that red-haired bundle of energy and fun could save Marsh from a lifetime of loneliness. Watching them now, oblivious to the world as newlyweds should be, Hal knew that he was right.

Who'd have believed that falling off a roof could result in so many happy endings? he mused. Not only had the accident provided him with the perfect excuse to wire Marsh, it had also put him in contact with Esther Rose.

Dear Esther Rose. How he loved her.

She was one in a million, the second Mrs. Roth—a woman who understood that a man couldn't necessarily stop loving his first wife just because she was dead.

A woman so special she didn't even want him to try.

* * * * *

HE'S MORE THAN
A MAN, HE'S
ONE OF OUR

HELP WANTED: DADDY
Carolyn Monroe

Newspaperman Boone Shelton thought he'd seen everything—until a couple of enterprising kids placed a classified ad to find a new husband for their unsuspecting mom. Then Boone found out "mom" was none other than his childhood dream girl, Nixie Cordaire Thomas! The children were ready to consider all applicants—especially fun-loving Boone. Now if he could just prove to Nixie he was the best man for the job....

Available in November from Silhouette Romance.

Fall in love with our **Fabulous Fathers!**

Silhouette
R O M A N C E™

Relive the romance...
Silhouette is proud to bring you

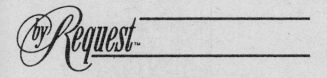

A program of collections of three complete
novels by the most requested authors
with the most requested themes.

Available in December:

Marriages in name only have a way of
leading to love....

Three complete novels in one special collection:

STRANGE ENCHANTMENT
by Annette Broadrick
MAIL-ORDER BRIDE by Debbie Macomber
THE DI MEDICI BRIDE
by Heather Graham Pozzessere

Available wherever Harlequin and
Silhouette books are sold.

THIS SIDE OF HEAVEN

The miracle of love is waiting to be discovered in Duncan, Oklahoma! Arlene James takes you there in her trilogy, THIS SIDE OF HEAVEN. Look for Book Three in November:

A WIFE WORTH WAITING FOR

Bolton Charles was too close for comfort. Clarice Revere was certainly grateful for the friendship he shared with her son. And she couldn't deny the man was attractive. But Clarice wasn't ready to trade her newfound freedom for love. Not yet. Maybe never. Bolton's patience was as limitless as his love—but could any man wait forever?

Available in November,
only from

Silhouette
ROMANCE™

Silhouette Books has done it again!

Opening night in October has never been as exciting! Come watch as the curtain rises and romance flourishes when the stars of tomorrow make their debuts today!

Revel in Jodi O'Donnell's STILL SWEET ON HIM—
Silhouette Romance #969
...as Callie Farrell's renovation of the family homestead leads her straight into the arms of teenage crush Drew Barnett!

Tingle with Carol Devine's BEAUTY AND THE BEASTMASTER—
Silhouette Desire #816
...as legal eagle Amanda Tarkington is carried off by wrestler Bram Masterson!

Thrill to Elyn Day's A BED OF ROSES—
Silhouette Special Edition #846
...as Dana Whitaker's body and soul are healed by sexy physical therapist Michael Gordon!

Believe when Kylie Brant's McLAIN'S LAW —
Silhouette Intimate Moments #528
...takes you into detective Connor McLain's life as he falls for psychic—and suspect—Michele Easton!

Catch the classics of tomorrow—*premiering* today—
only from ❤ *Silhouette*

**And now for
something completely different
from Silhouette....**

SPELLBOUND
R O M A N C E

Every once in a while, Silhouette brings you a
book that is truly unique and innovative, taking
you into the world of paranormal happenings.
And now these stories will carry our special
"Spellbound" flash, letting you know that you're
in for a truly exciting reading experience!

In October, look for *McLain's Law* (IM #528)
by Kylie Brant

Lieutenant Detective Connor McLain believes
only in what he can see—until Michele Easton's
haunting visions help him solve a case...and her
love opens his heart!

McLain's Law is also the Intimate Moments
"Premiere" title, introducing you to a debut
author, sure to be the star of tomorrow!

Available in October...only from
Silhouette Intimate Moments

TAKE A WALK ON THE
DARK SIDE OF LOVE WITH

October is the shivery season, when chill winds blow and
shadows walk the night. Come along with us into a haunting
world where love and danger go hand in hand, where
passions will thrill you and dangers will chill you. Silhouette's
second annual collection from the dark side of love brings
you three perfectly haunting tales from three of our most
bewitching authors:

Kathleen Korbel
Carla Cassidy
Lori Herter

Haunting a store near you this October.

Only from  where passion lives.

SILHOUETTE.... Where Passion Lives

Don't miss these Silhouette favorites by some of our most popular authors!
And now, you can receive a discount by ordering two or more titles!

Silhouette Desire®

#05751	THE MAN WITH THE MIDNIGHT EYES BJ James	$2.89	☐
#05763	THE COWBOY Cait London	$2.89	☐
#05774	TENNESSEE WALTZ Jackie Merritt	$2.89	☐
#05779	THE RANCHER AND THE RUNAWAY BRIDE Joan Johnston	$2.89	☐

Silhouette Intimate Moments®

#07417	WOLF AND THE ANGEL Kathleen Creighton	$3.29	☐
#07480	DIAMOND WILLOW Kathleen Eagle	$3.39	☐
#07486	MEMORIES OF LAURA Marilyn Pappano	$3.39	☐
#07493	QUINN EISLEY'S WAR Patricia Gardner Evans	$3.39	☐

Silhouette Shadows®

#27003	STRANGER IN THE MIST Lee Karr	$3.50	☐
#27007	FLASHBACK Terri Herrington	$3.50	☐
#27009	BREAK THE NIGHT Anne Stuart	$3.50	☐
#27012	DARK ENCHANTMENT Jane Toombs	$3.50	☐

Silhouette Special Edition®

#09754	THERE AND NOW Linda Lael Miller	$3.39	☐
#09770	FATHER: UNKNOWN Andrea Edwards	$3.39	☐
#09791	THE CAT THAT LIVED ON PARK AVENUE Tracy Sinclair	$3.39	☐
#09811	HE'S THE RICH BOY Lisa Jackson	$3.39	☐

Silhouette Romance®

#08893	LETTERS FROM HOME Toni Collins	$2.69	☐
#08915	NEW YEAR'S BABY Stella Bagwell	$2.69	☐
#08927	THE PURSUIT OF HAPPINESS Anne Peters	$2.69	☐
#08952	INSTANT FATHER Lucy Gordon	$2.75	☐

	AMOUNT	$ _____
DEDUCT:	10% DISCOUNT FOR 2+ BOOKS	$ _____
	POSTAGE & HANDLING	$ _____
	($1.00 for one book, 50¢ for each additional)	
	APPLICABLE TAXES*	$ _____
	TOTAL PAYABLE	$ _____
	(check or money order—please do not send cash)	

To order, complete this form and send it, along with a check or money order for the total above, payable to Silhouette Books, to: *In the U.S.*: 3010 Walden Avenue, P.O. Box 9077, Buffalo, NY 14269-9077; *In Canada*: P.O. Box 636, Fort Erie, Ontario, L2A 5X3.

Name: _____

Address: _____ City: _____

State/Prov.: _____ Zip/Postal Code: _____

*New York residents remit applicable sales taxes.
Canadian residents remit applicable GST and provincial taxes.

SBACK-OD

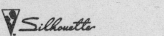